JAKE MADDOX
GRAPHIC NOVELS

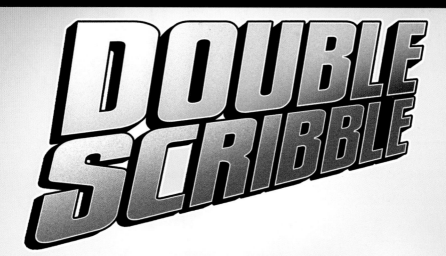

DOUBLE SCRIBBLE

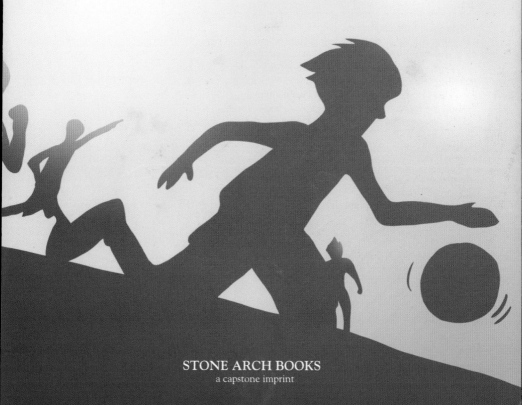

STONE ARCH BOOKS

a capstone imprint

JAKE MADDOX
GRAPHIC NOVELS

Jake Maddox Graphic Novels are published by
Stone Arch Books, a Capstone imprint
1710 Roe Crest Drive
North Mankato, Minnesota 56003

www.mycapstone.com

Library of Congress Cataloging-in-Publication Data
is available on the Library of Congress website.

ISBN: 978-1-4965-3701-0 (library binding)
ISBN: 978-1-4965-3705-8 (paperback)
ISBN: 978-1-4965-3721-8 (ebook PDF)

Summary: Diego "Clutch" Rivera became the
school's hero when he made the game-winning
hook shot to take home last season's championship
trophy. With the new season beginning, expectations
are high that Clutch will lead the basketball team
to another title. But when his trademark hook shot
clanks off the rim, Diego's world crashes back to
reality. He's stuck in a slump, and the only way to
work out his problems is to draw out his thoughts
and feelings in his sketchbook. Will Diego be able to
get his head back in the game and help his team win
another championship?

Editor: Aaron Sautter
Designer: Brann Garvey
Production: Gene Bentdahl

Printed in the United States of America.
010044S17

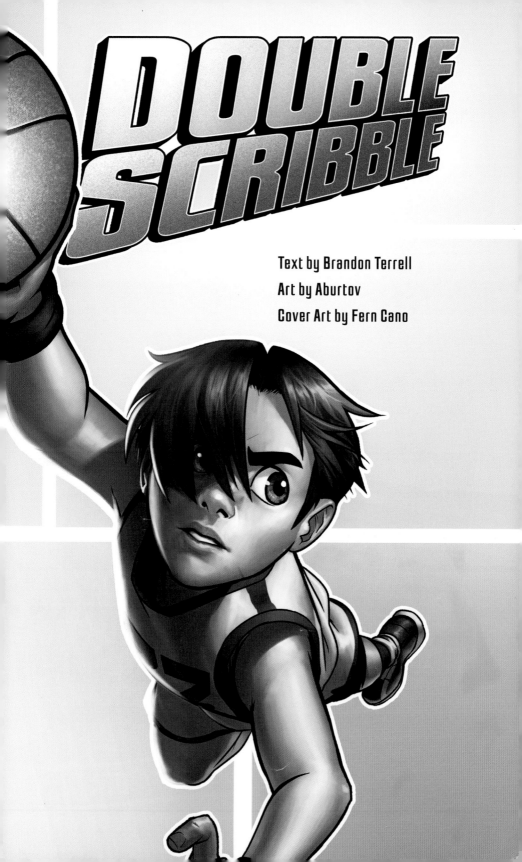

DOUBLE SCRIBBLE

Text by Brandon Terrell

Art by Aburtov

Cover Art by Fern Cano

STARTING LINEUP

C

33

DIEGO RIVERA

PG

15

MALCOLM DOWNS

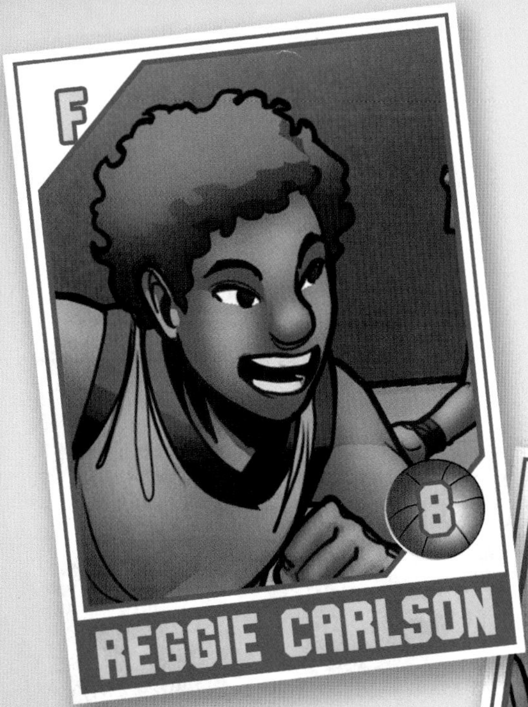
F
8
REGGIE CARLSON

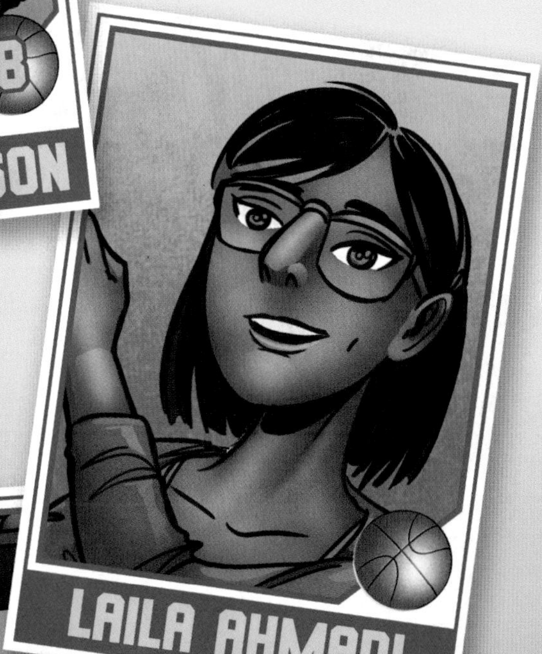
LAILA AHMADI

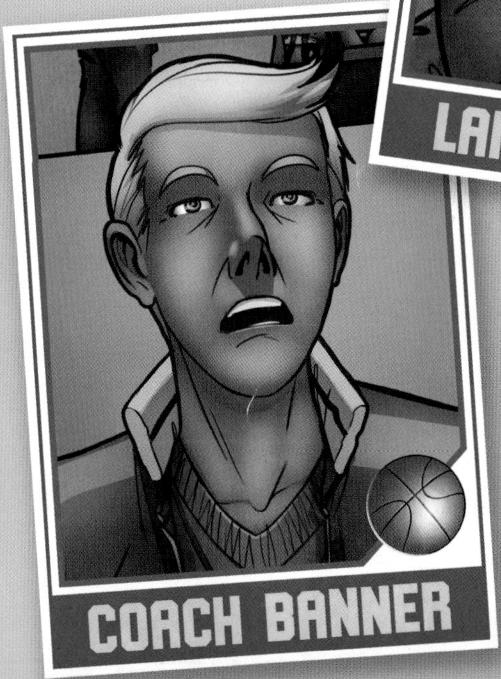
COACH BANNER

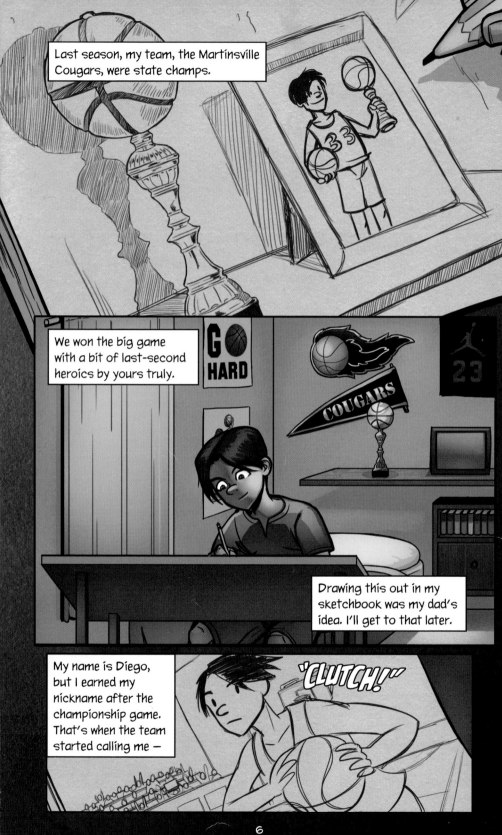

Last season, my team, the Martinsville Cougars, were state champs.

We won the big game with a bit of last-second heroics by yours truly.

Drawing this out in my sketchbook was my dad's idea. I'll get to that later.

My name is Diego, but I earned my nickname after the championship game. That's when the team started calling me —

"CLUTCH!"

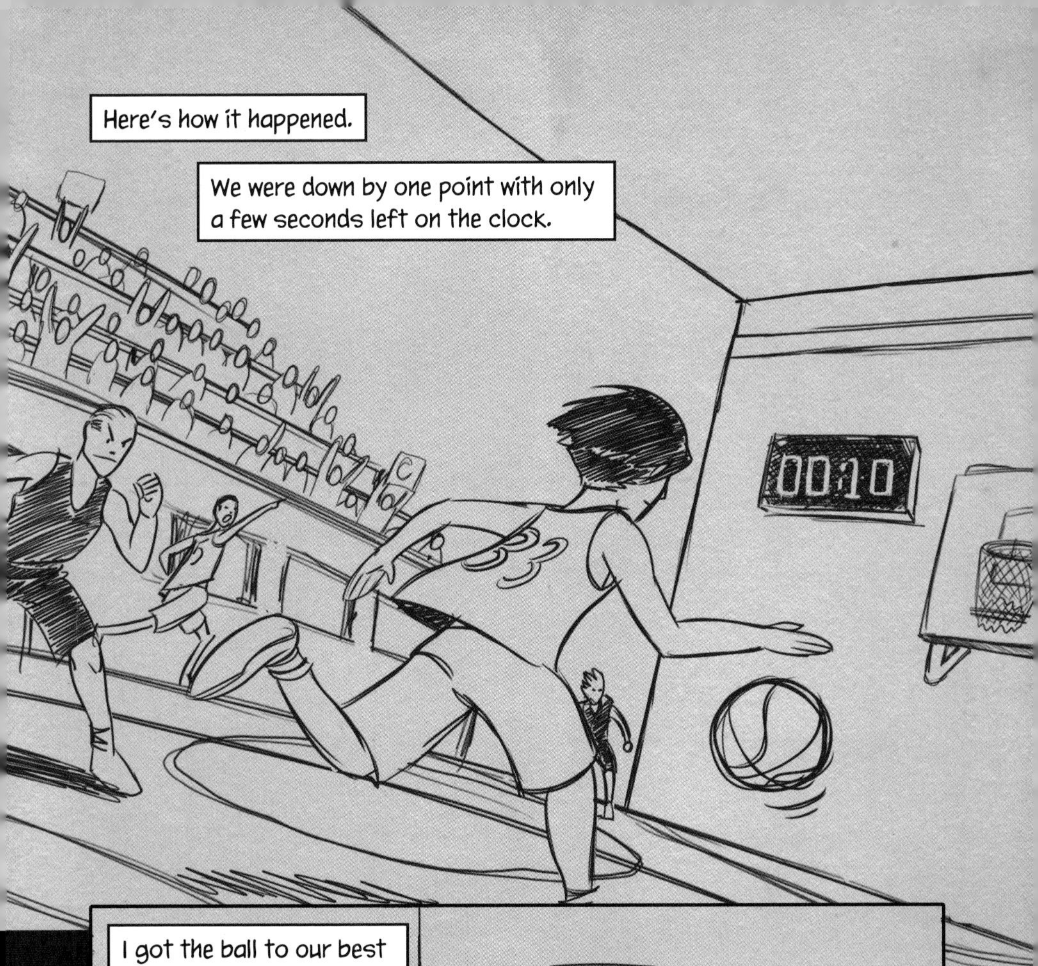
Here's how it happened.
We were down by one point with only a few seconds left on the clock.
00:10
33

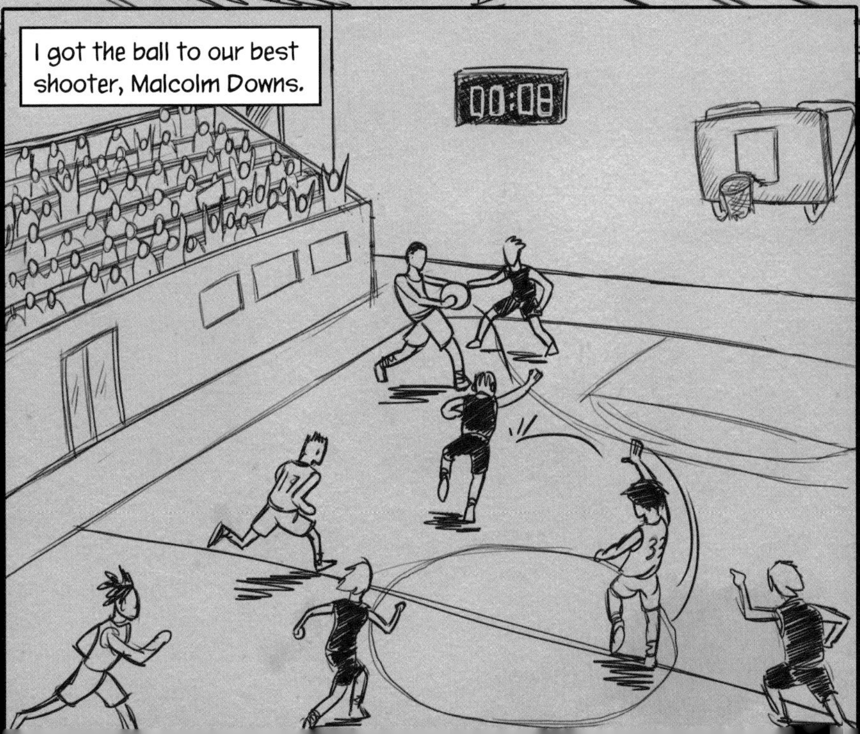
I got the ball to our best shooter, Malcolm Downs.
00:08
17
33

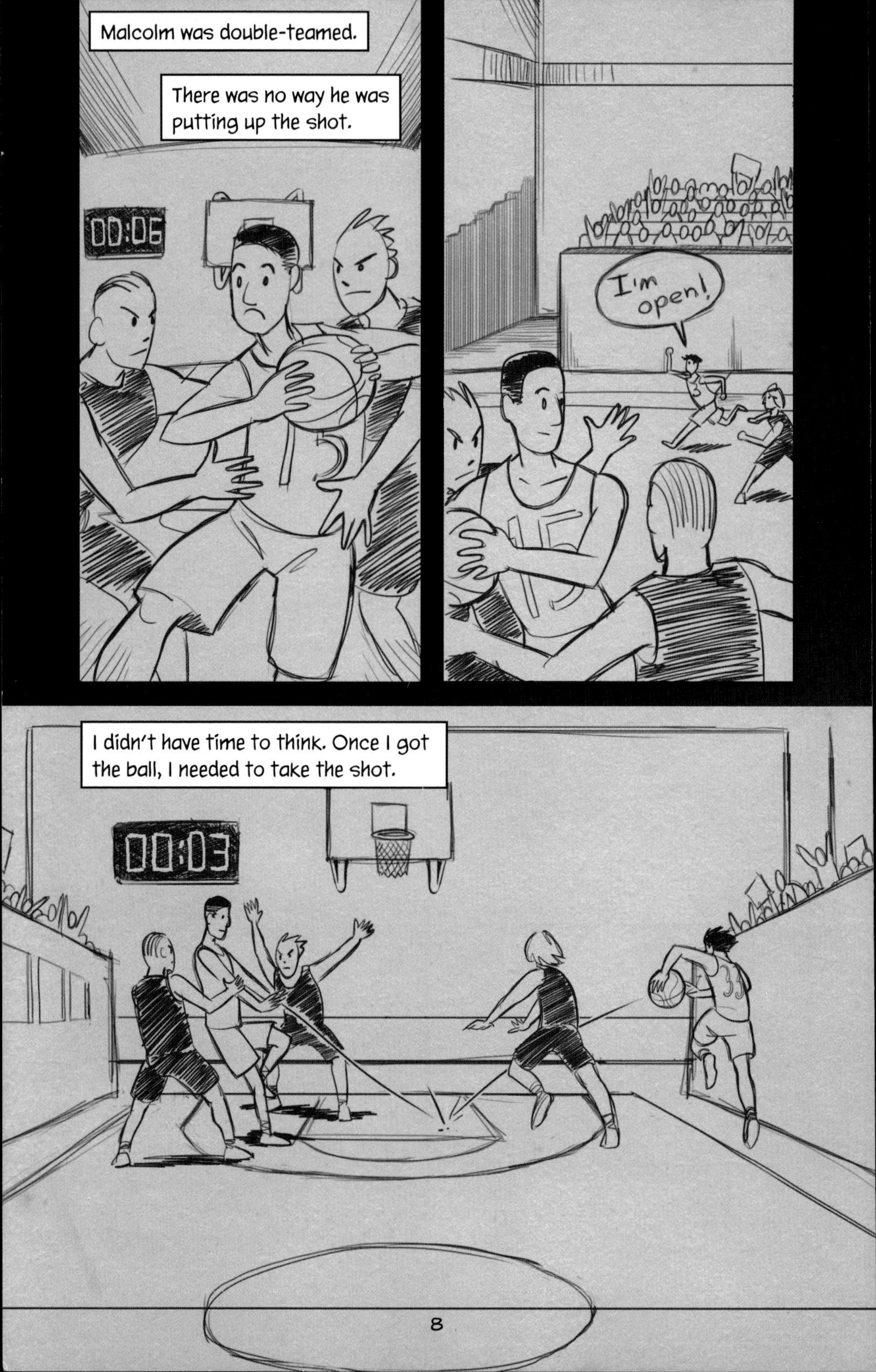
Malcolm was double-teamed.
There was no way he was putting up the shot.
00:06
I'm open!
I didn't have time to think. Once I got the ball, I needed to take the shot.
00:03

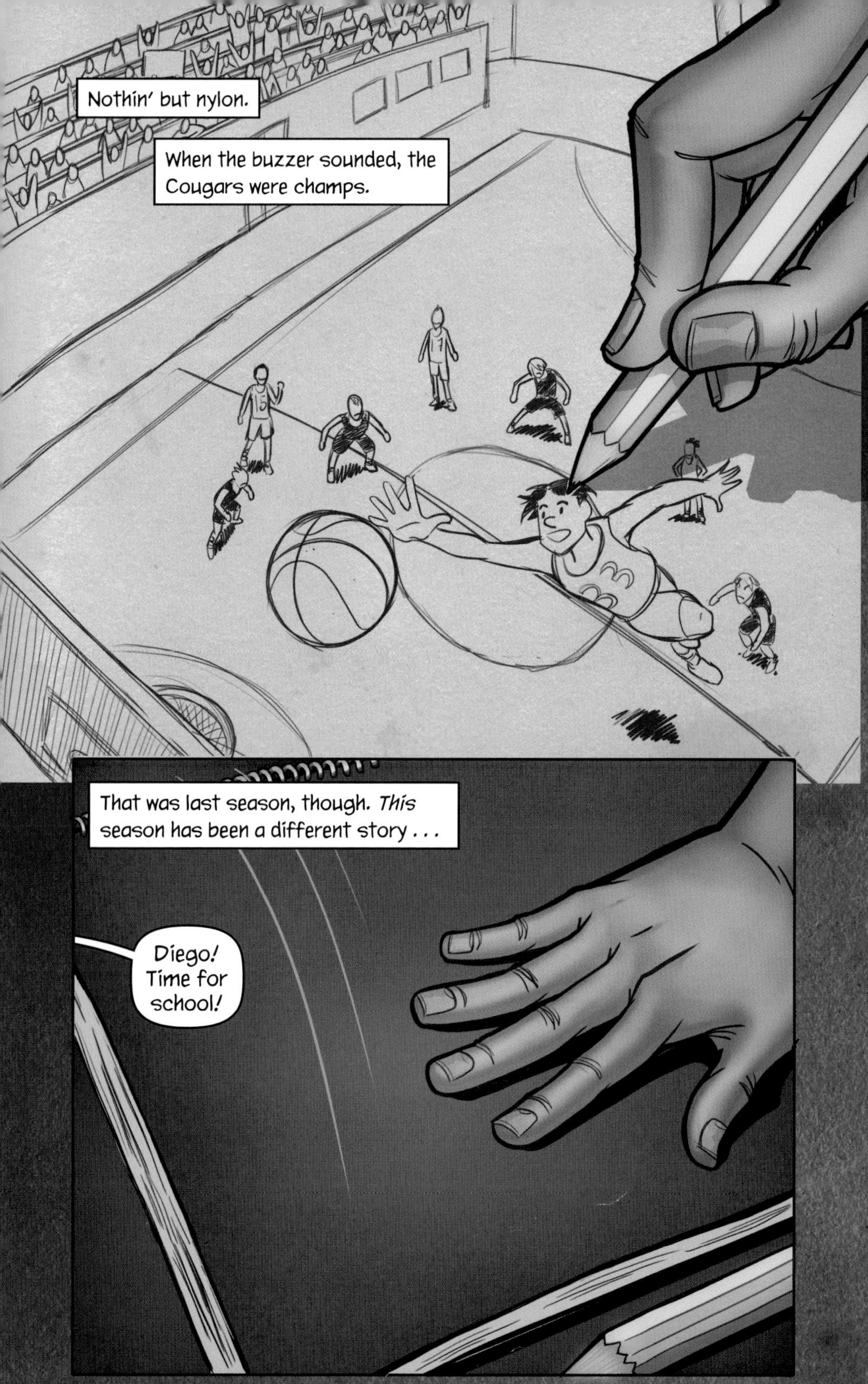
Nothin' but nylon.
When the buzzer sounded, the Cougars were champs.
That was last season, though. *This* season has been a different story . . .
Diego! Time for school!

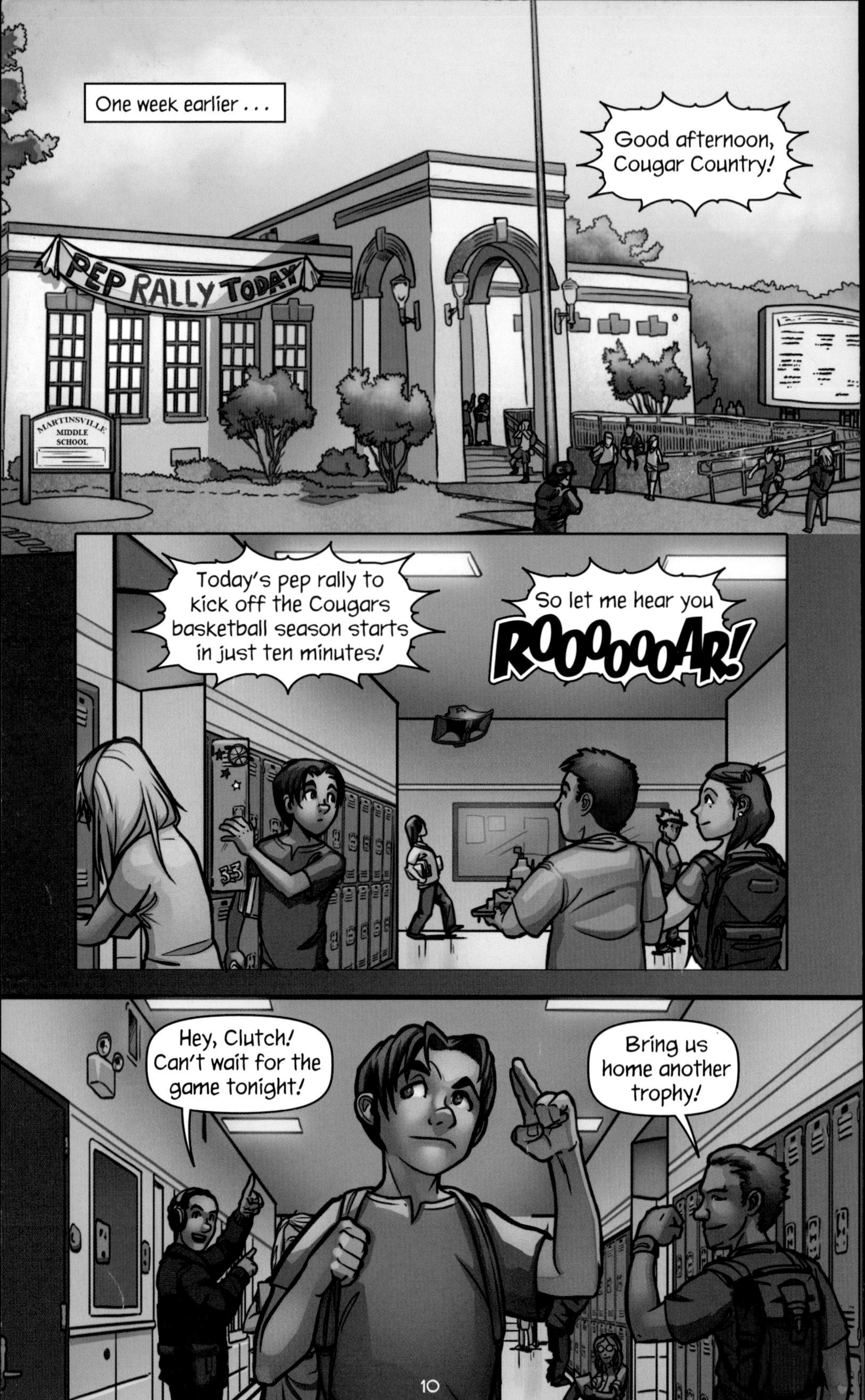
One week earlier . . .
Good afternoon, Cougar Country!
PEP RALLY TODAY
MARTINSVILLE MIDDLE SCHOOL
Today's pep rally to kick off the Cougars basketball season starts in just ten minutes!
So let me hear you
ROOOOOOAR!
Hey, Clutch! Can't wait for the game tonight!
Bring us home another trophy!

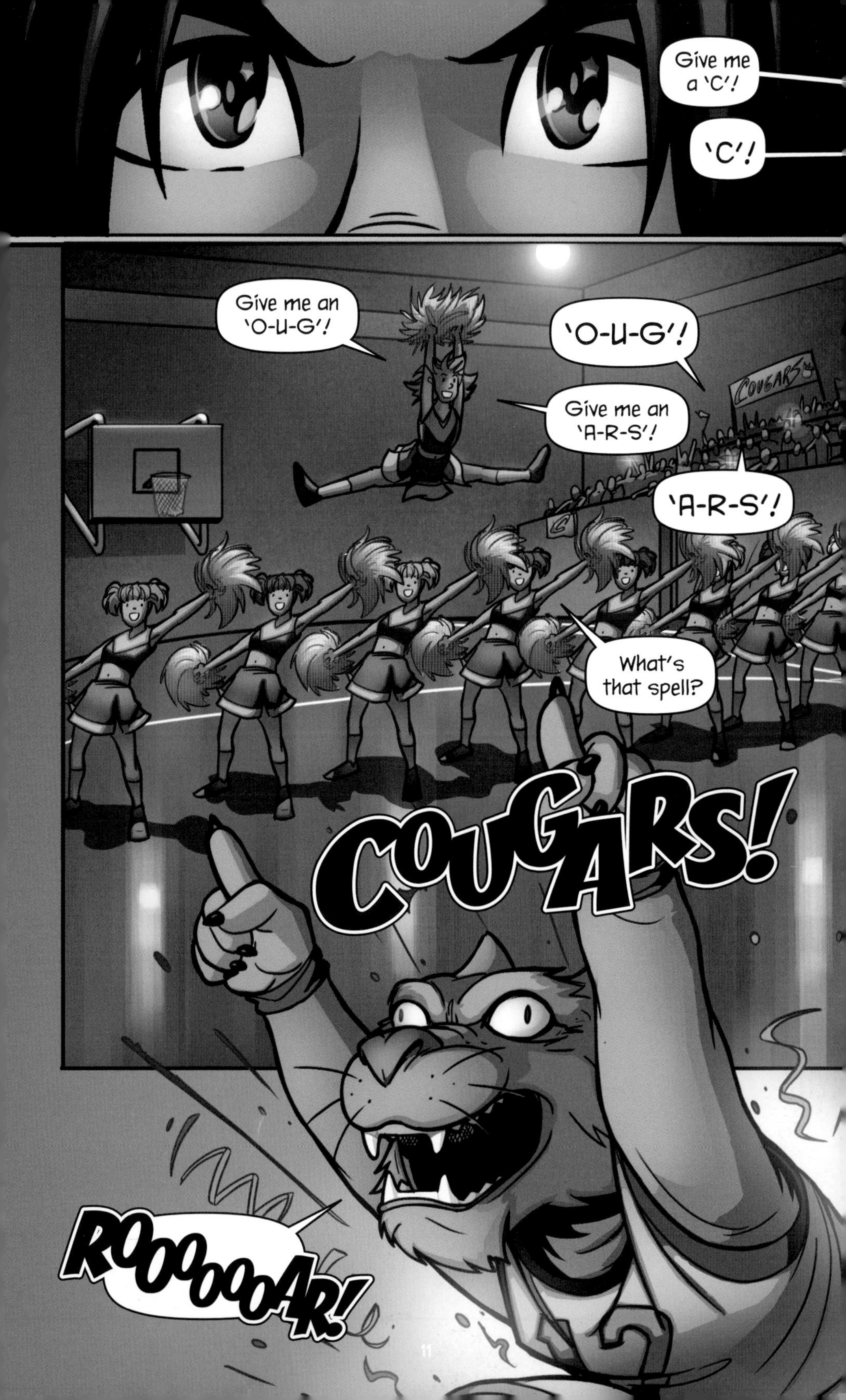
Give me a 'C'!
'C'!
Give me an 'O-U-G'!
'O-U-G'!
Give me an 'A-R-S'!
'A-R-S'!
What's that spell?
COUGARS!
ROOOOOOOAR!

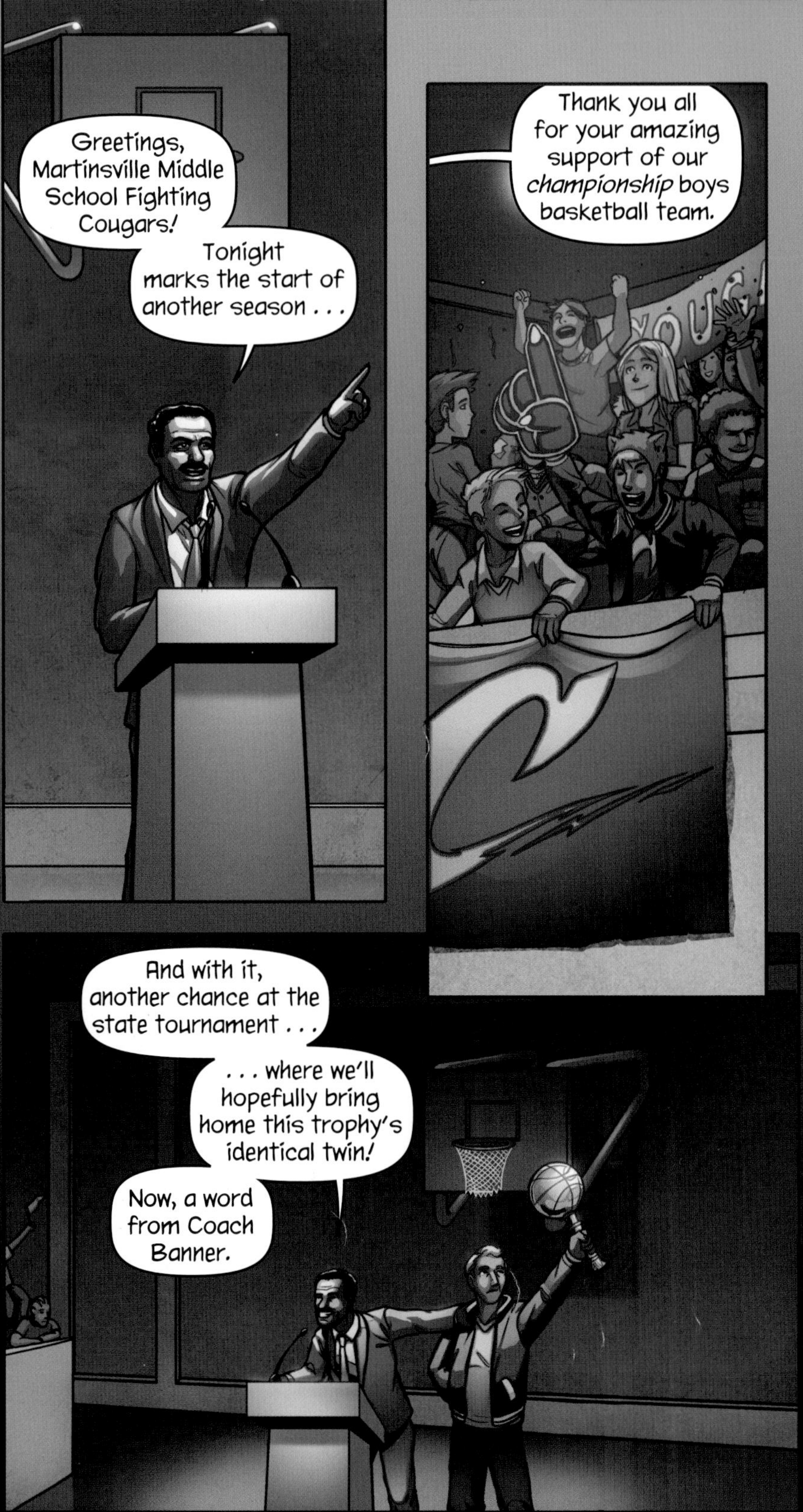
Greetings, Martinsville Middle School Fighting Cougars!
Tonight marks the start of another season . . .
Thank you all for your amazing support of our *championship* boys basketball team.
And with it, another chance at the state tournament . . .
. . . where we'll hopefully bring home this trophy's identical twin!
Now, a word from Coach Banner.

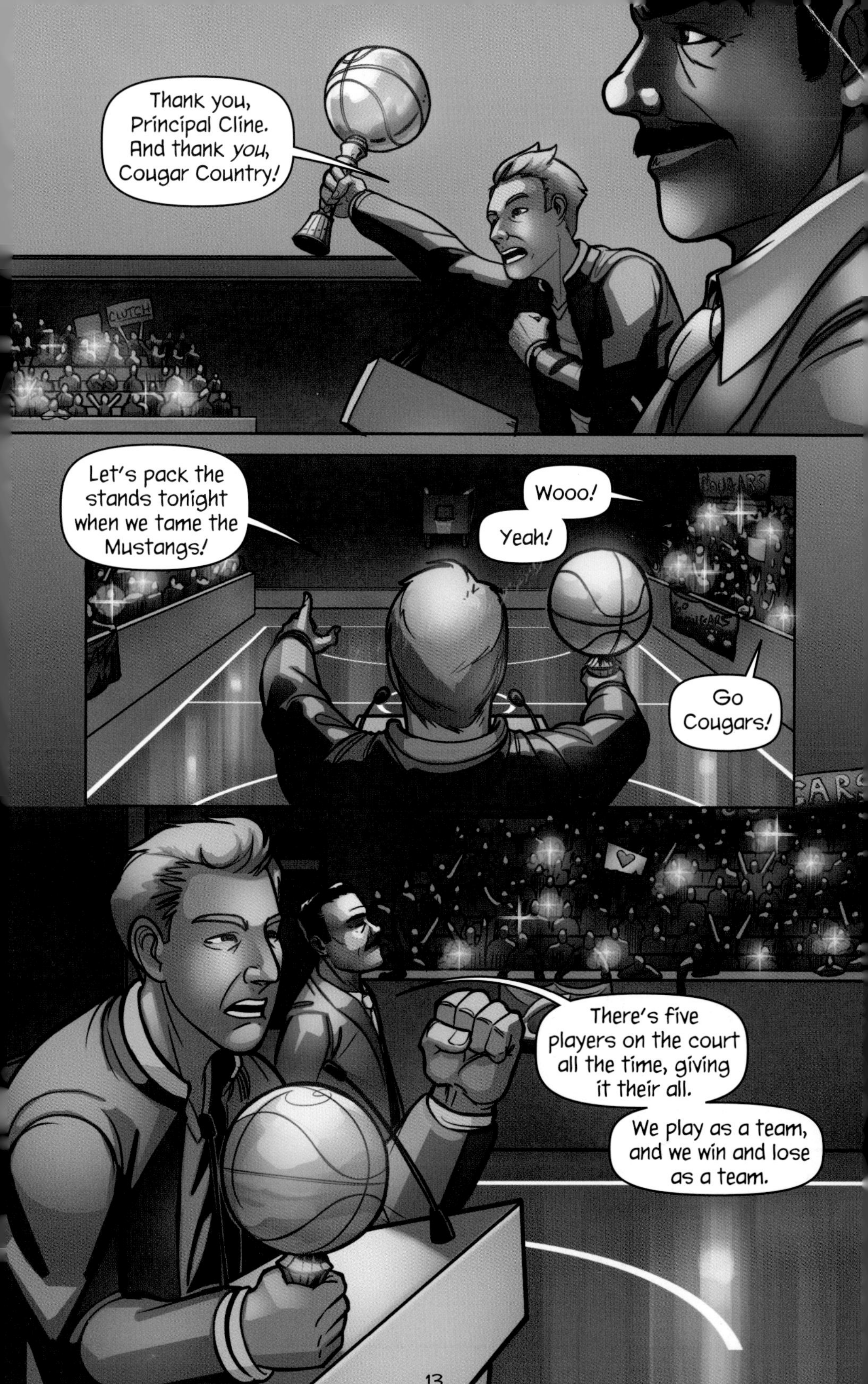
Thank you, Principal Cline. And thank *you*, Cougar Country!
CLUTCH
Let's pack the stands tonight when we tame the Mustangs!
Wooo!
Yeah!
COUGARS
GO COUGARS
Go Cougars!
There's five players on the court all the time, giving it their all.
We play as a team, and we win and lose as a team.

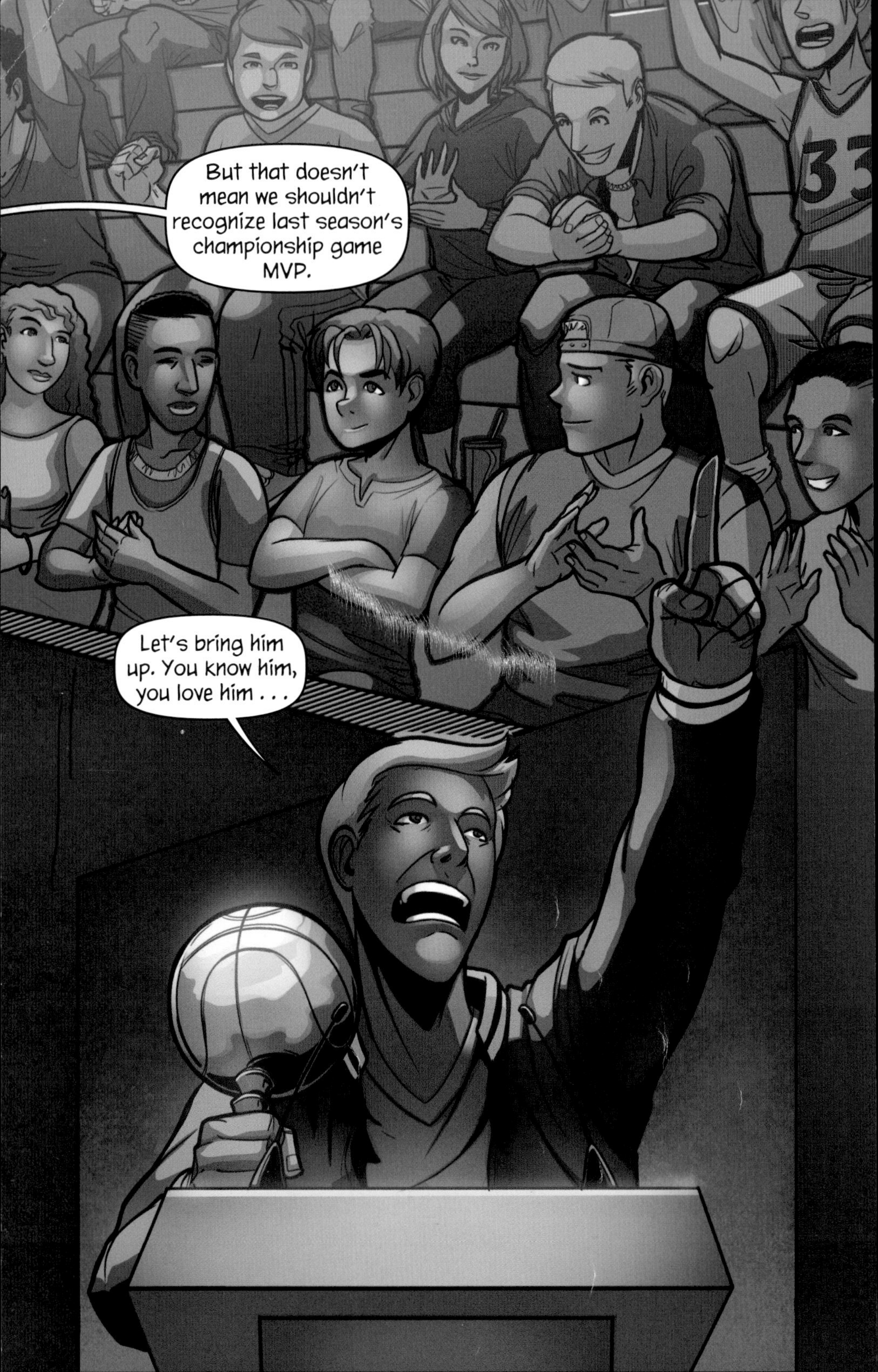
But that doesn't mean we shouldn't recognize last season's championship game MVP.
33
Let's bring him up. You know him, you love him . . .

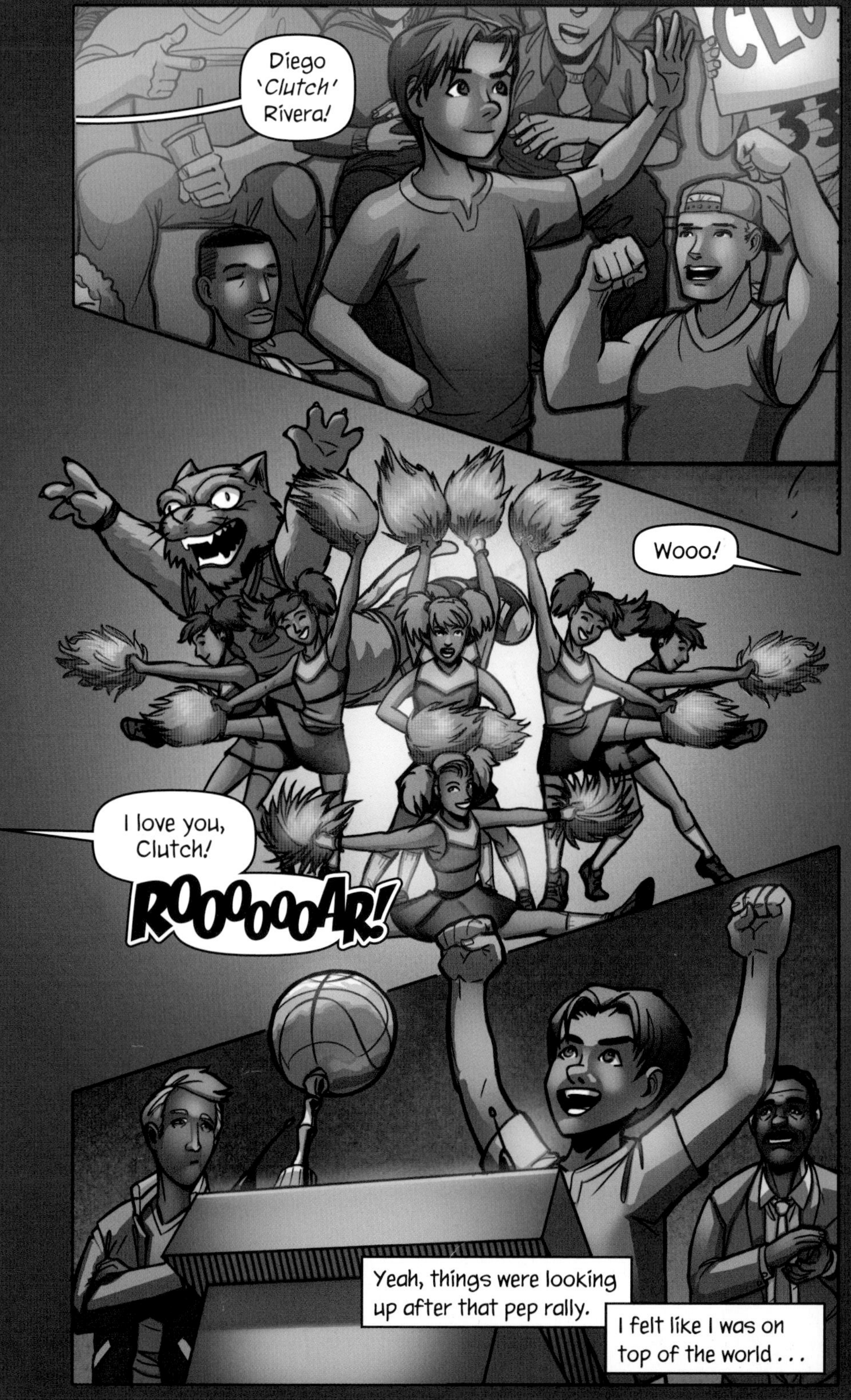
Diego 'Clutch' Rivera!
Wooo!
I love you, Clutch!
ROOOOOOOAR!
Yeah, things were looking up after that pep rally.
I felt like I was on top of the world . . .

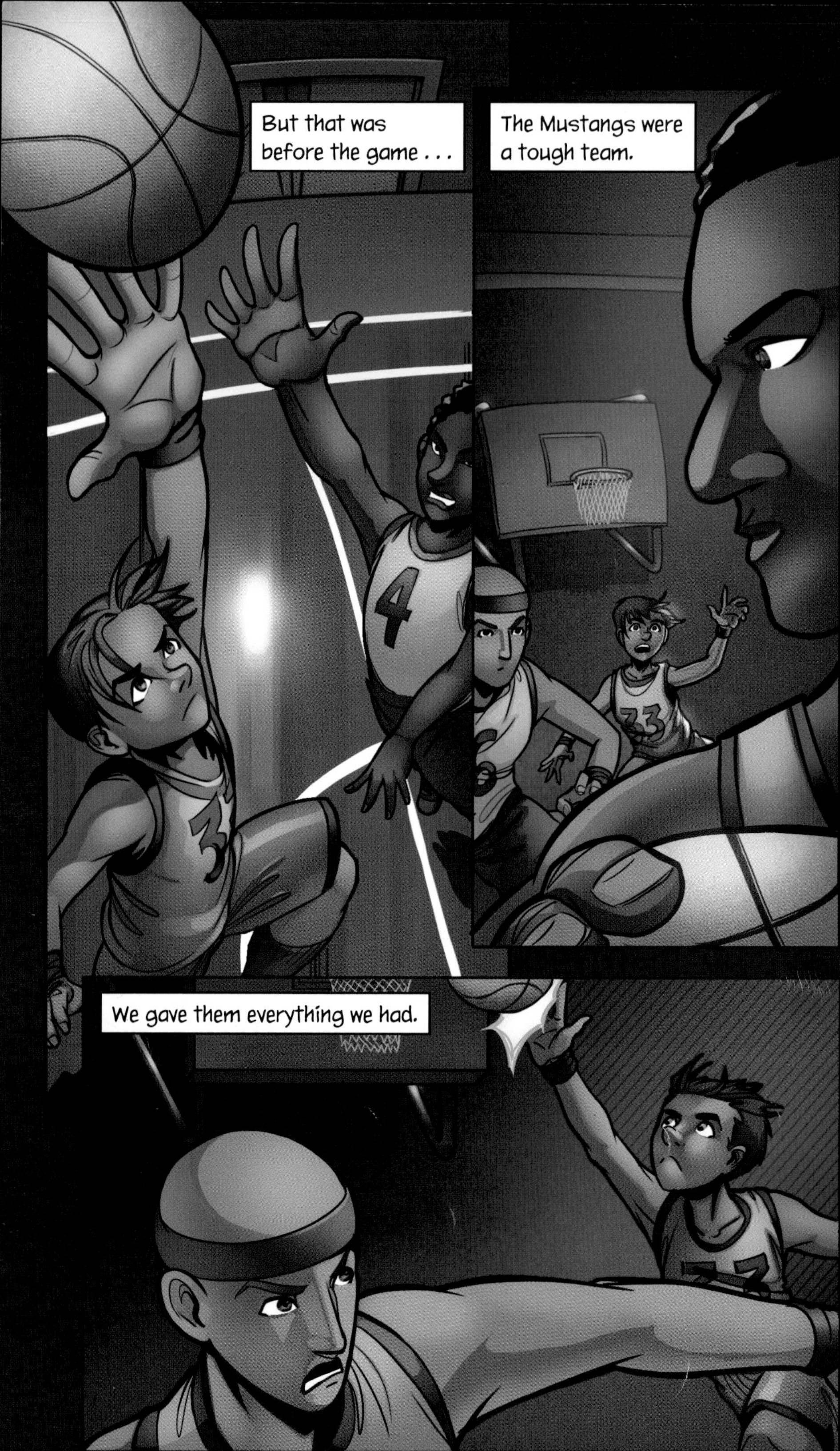
But that was before the game . . .
The Mustangs were a tough team.
We gave them everything we had.

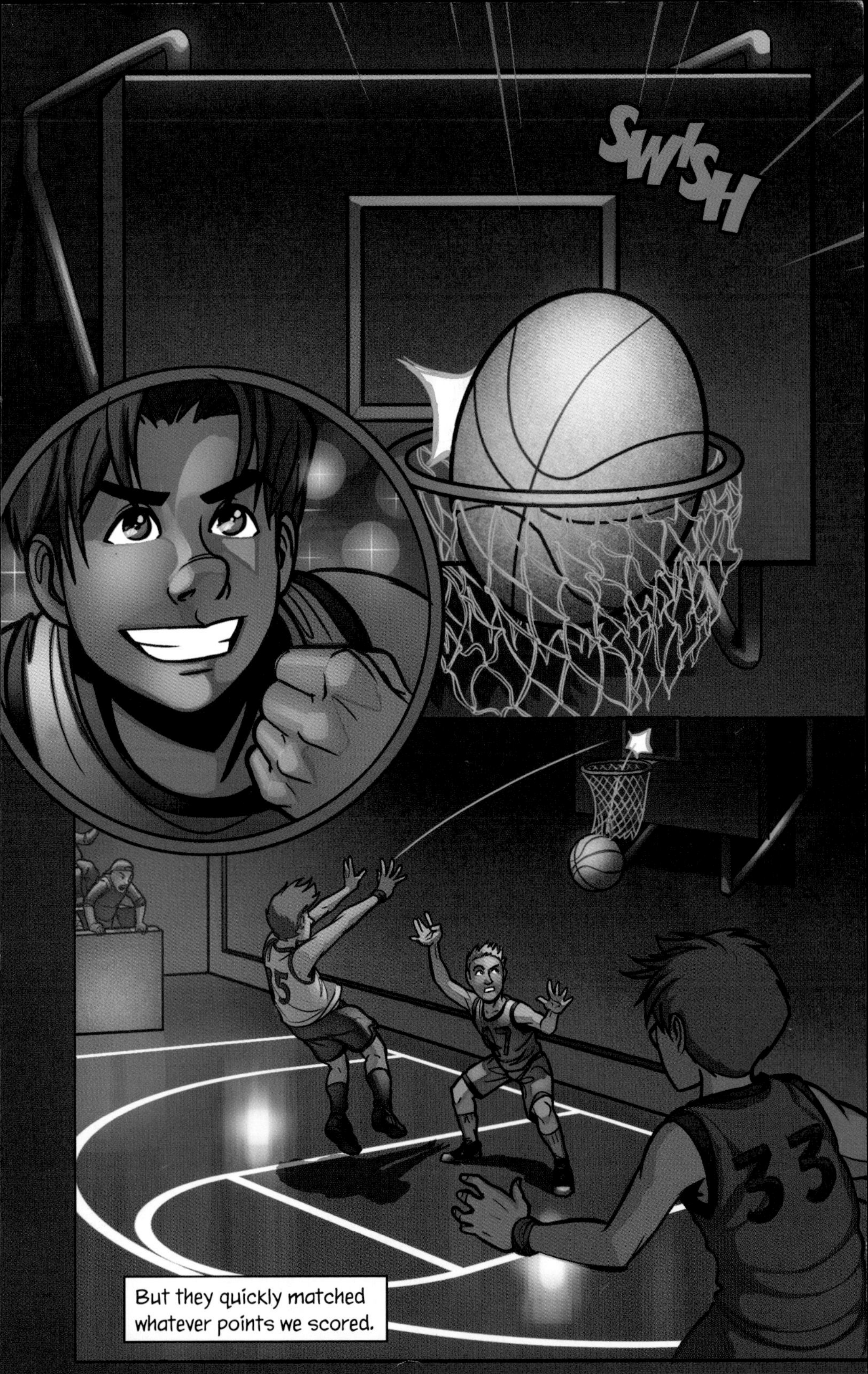
SWISH
But they quickly matched whatever points we scored.

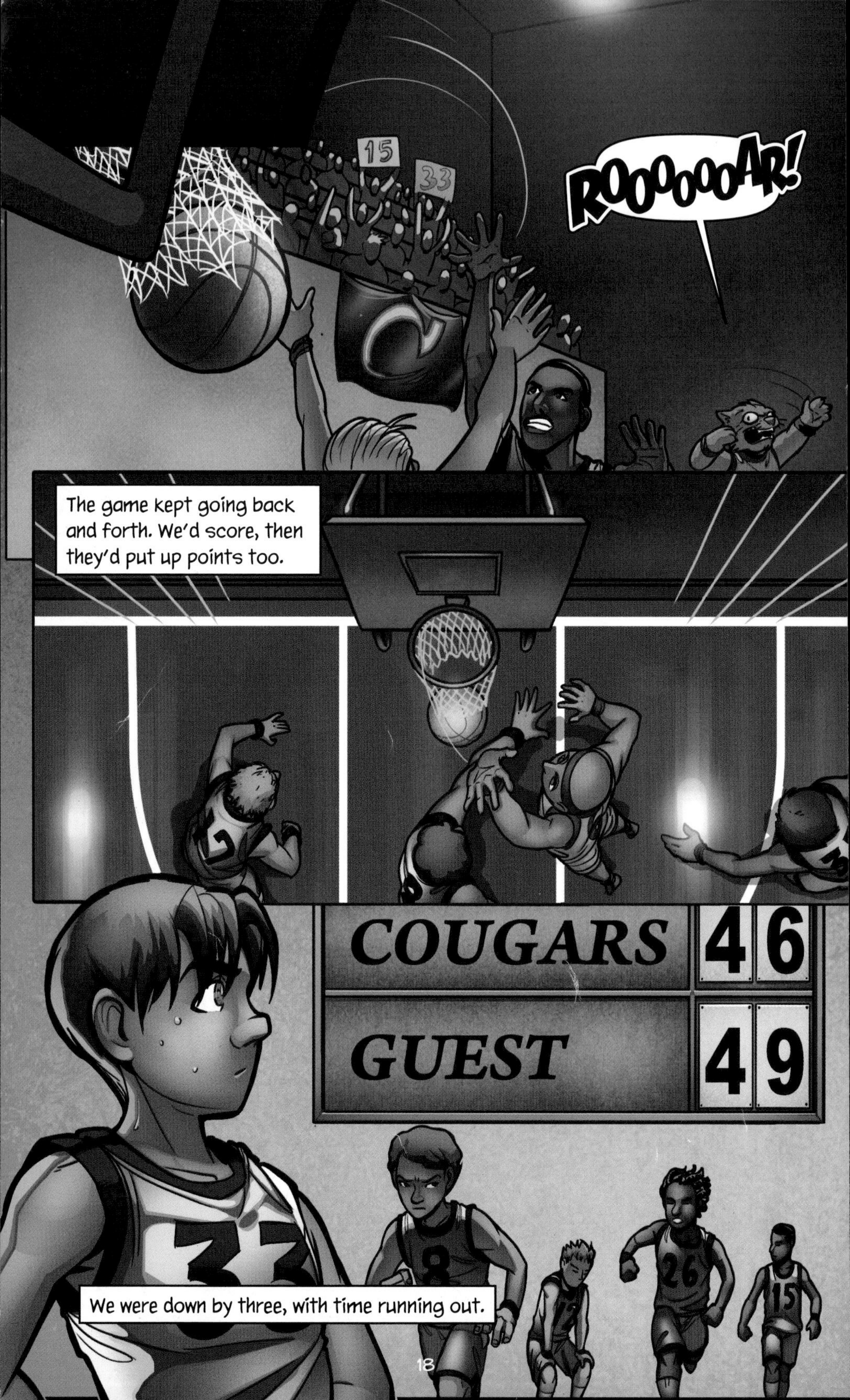
15
33
ROOOOOOOAR!
The game kept going back and forth. We'd score, then they'd put up points too.
COUGARS 46
GUEST 49
We were down by three, with time running out.

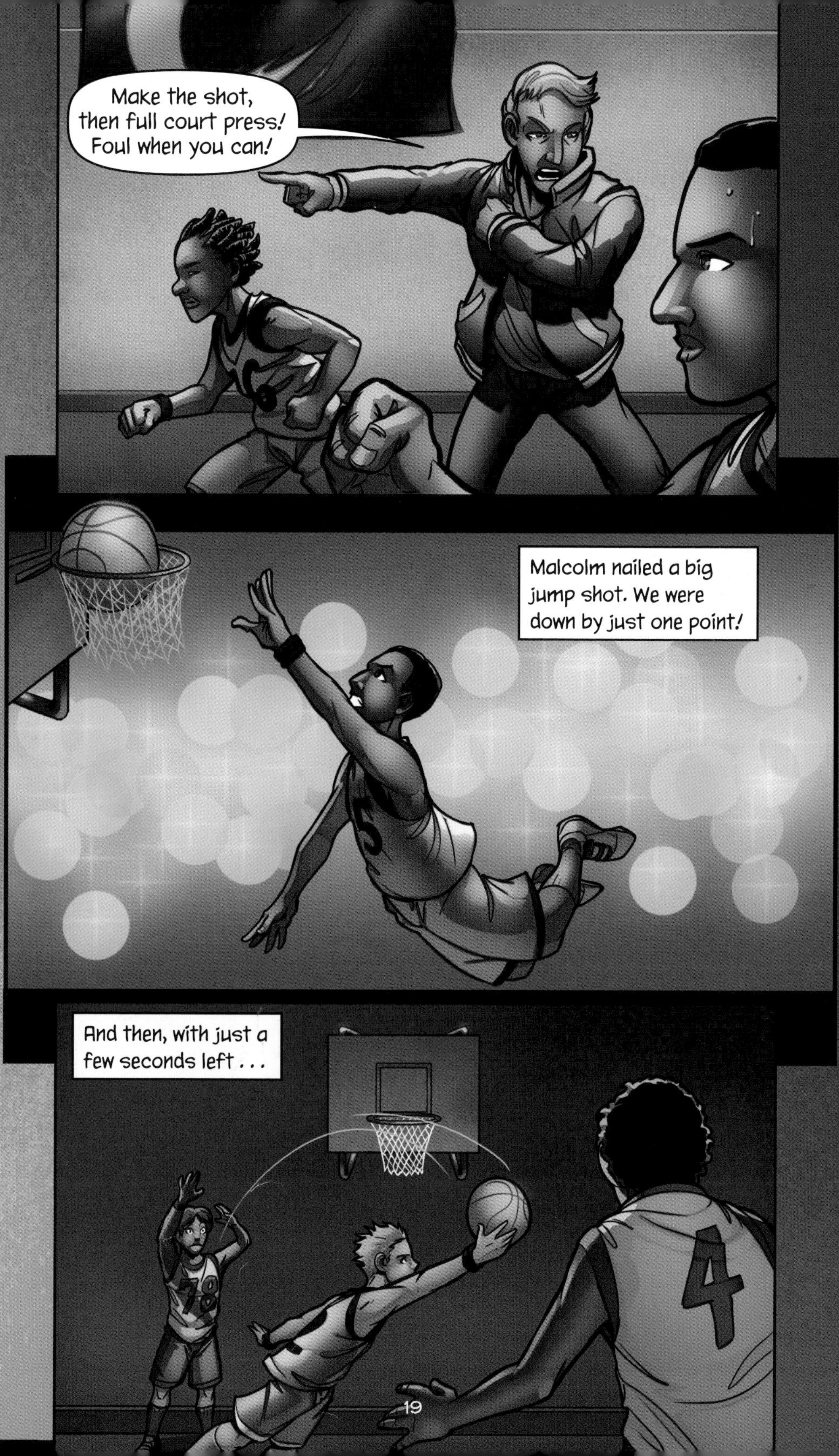
Make the shot, then full court press! Foul when you can!
Malcolm nailed a big jump shot. We were down by just one point!
And then, with just a few seconds left . . .

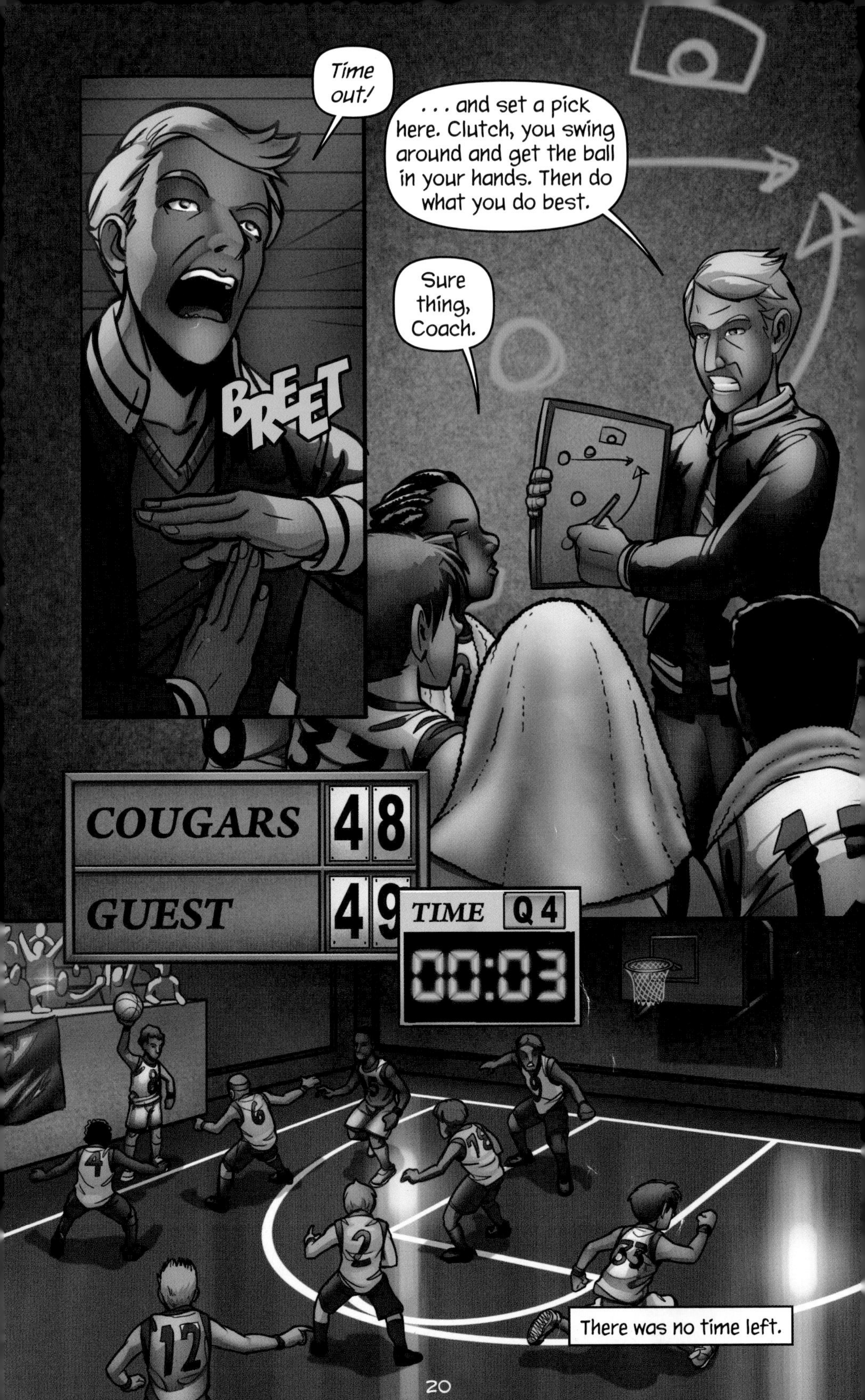
Time out!
BREET
. . . and set a pick here. Clutch, you swing around and get the ball in your hands. Then do what you do best.
Sure thing, Coach.
COUGARS 48
GUEST 49
TIME Q4
00:03
There was no time left.

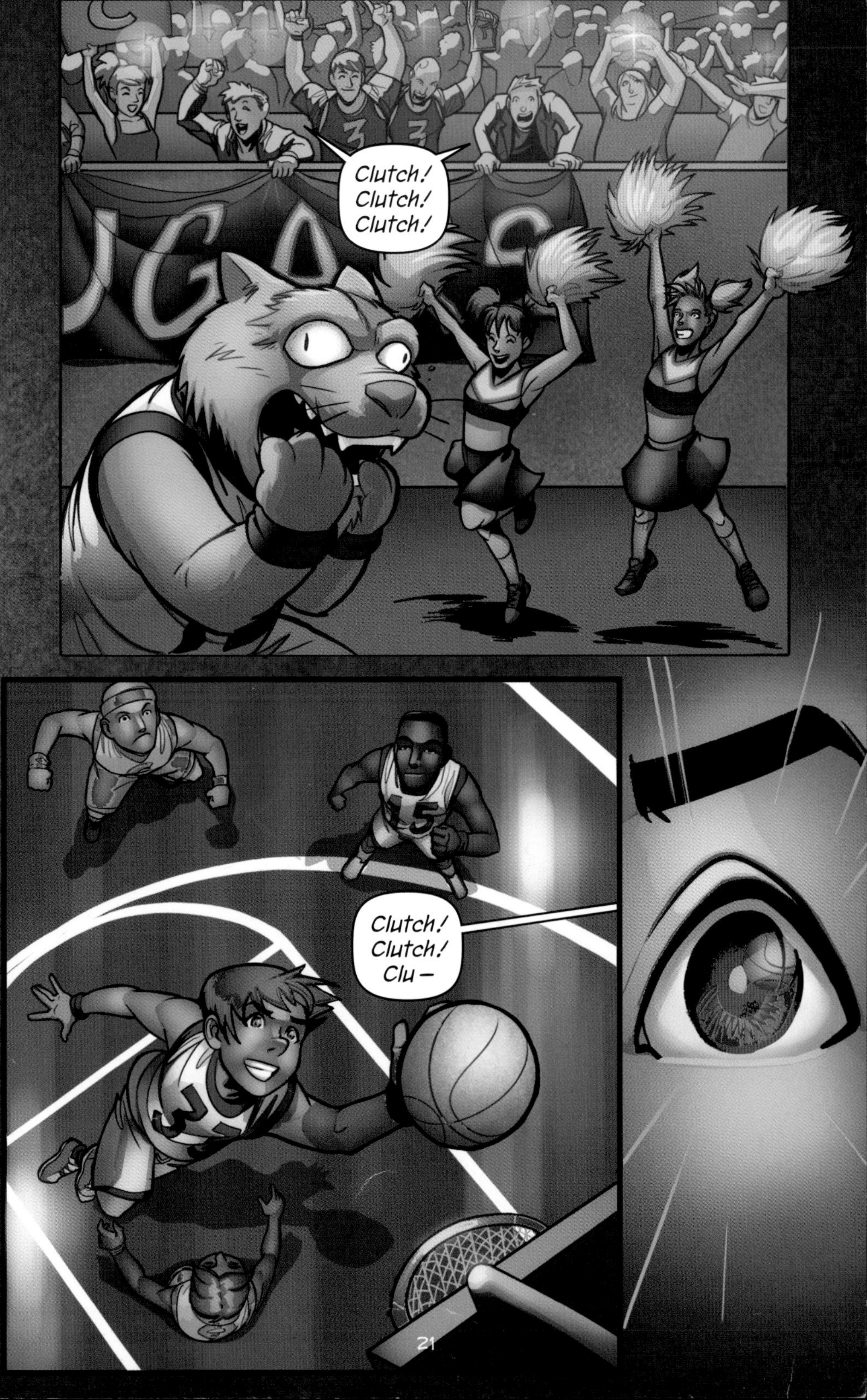
Clutch! Clutch! Clutch!
Clutch! Clutch! Clu—

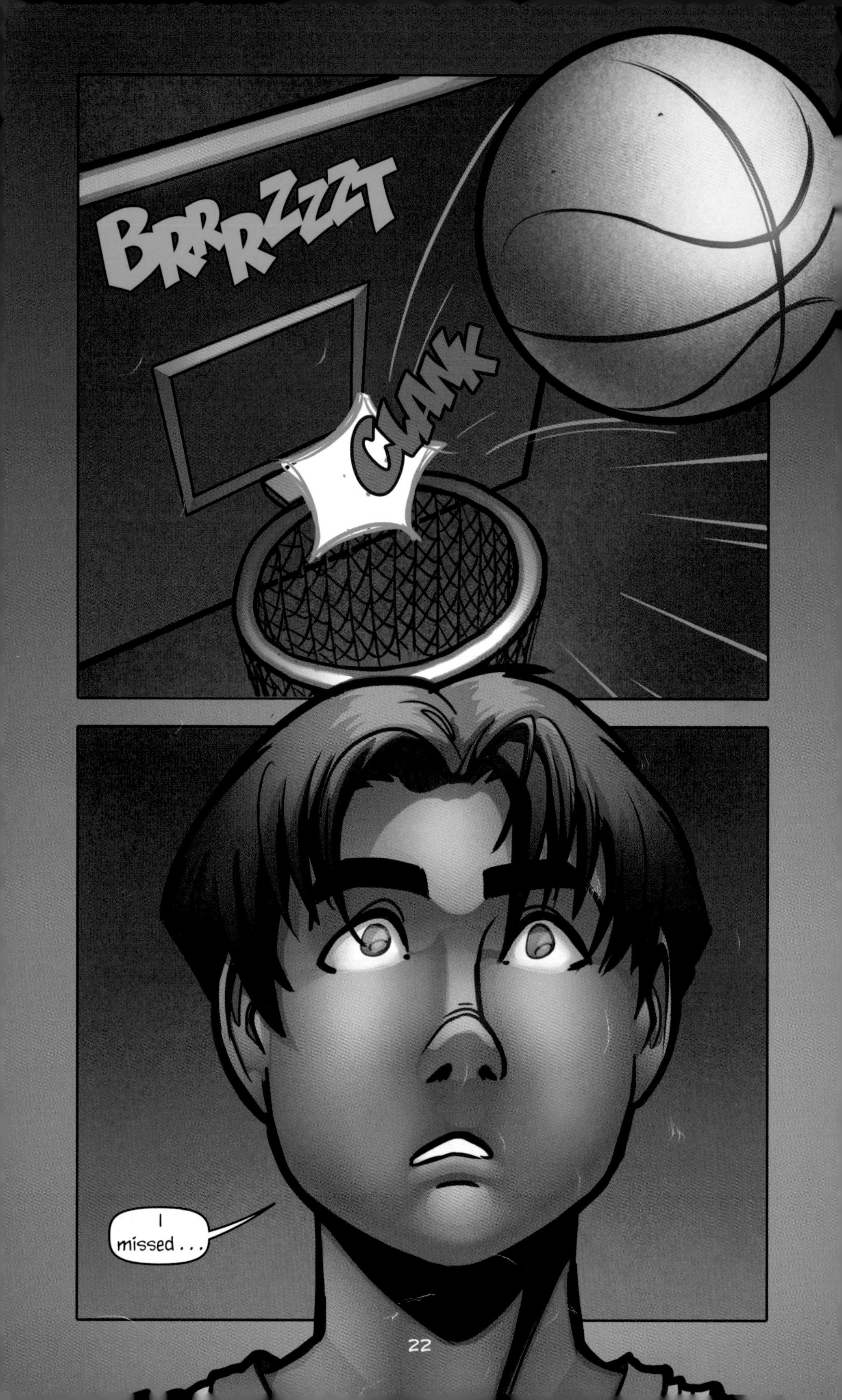
BRRRZZZT
CLANK
I missed . . .

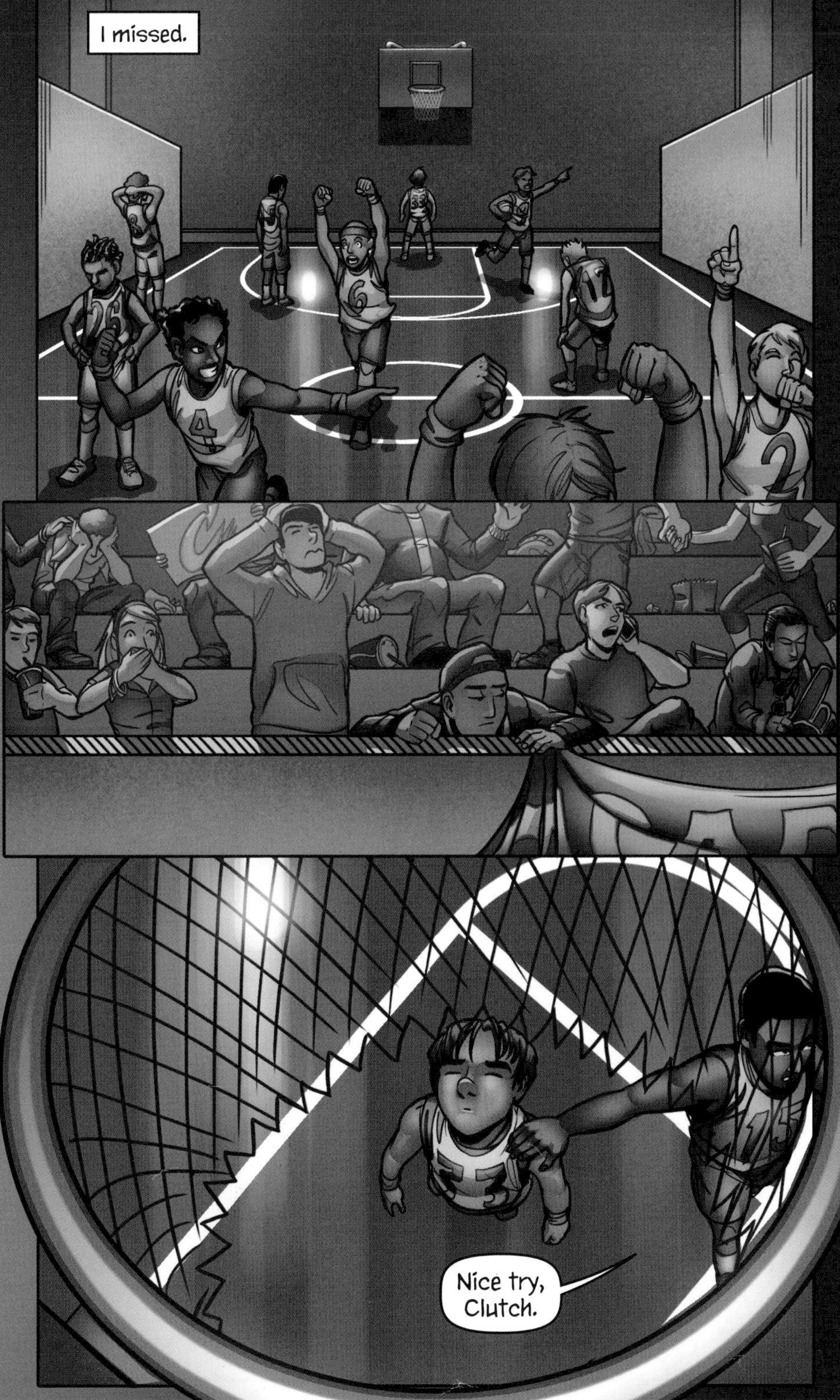
I missed.
Nice try, Clutch.

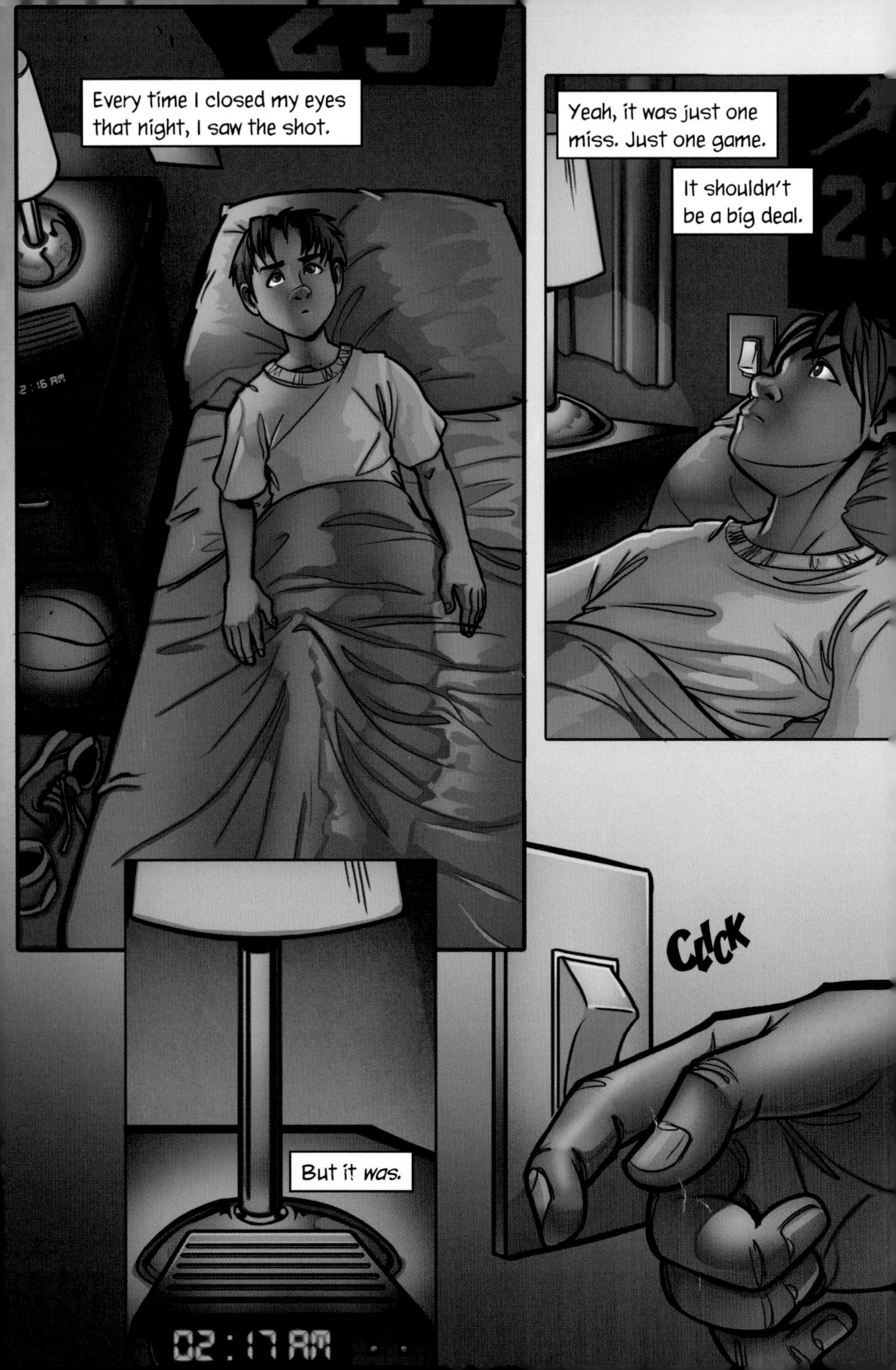
Every time I closed my eyes that night, I saw the shot.
Yeah, it was just one miss. Just one game.
It shouldn't be a big deal.
2:16 AM
But it *was*.
02:17 AM
CLICK

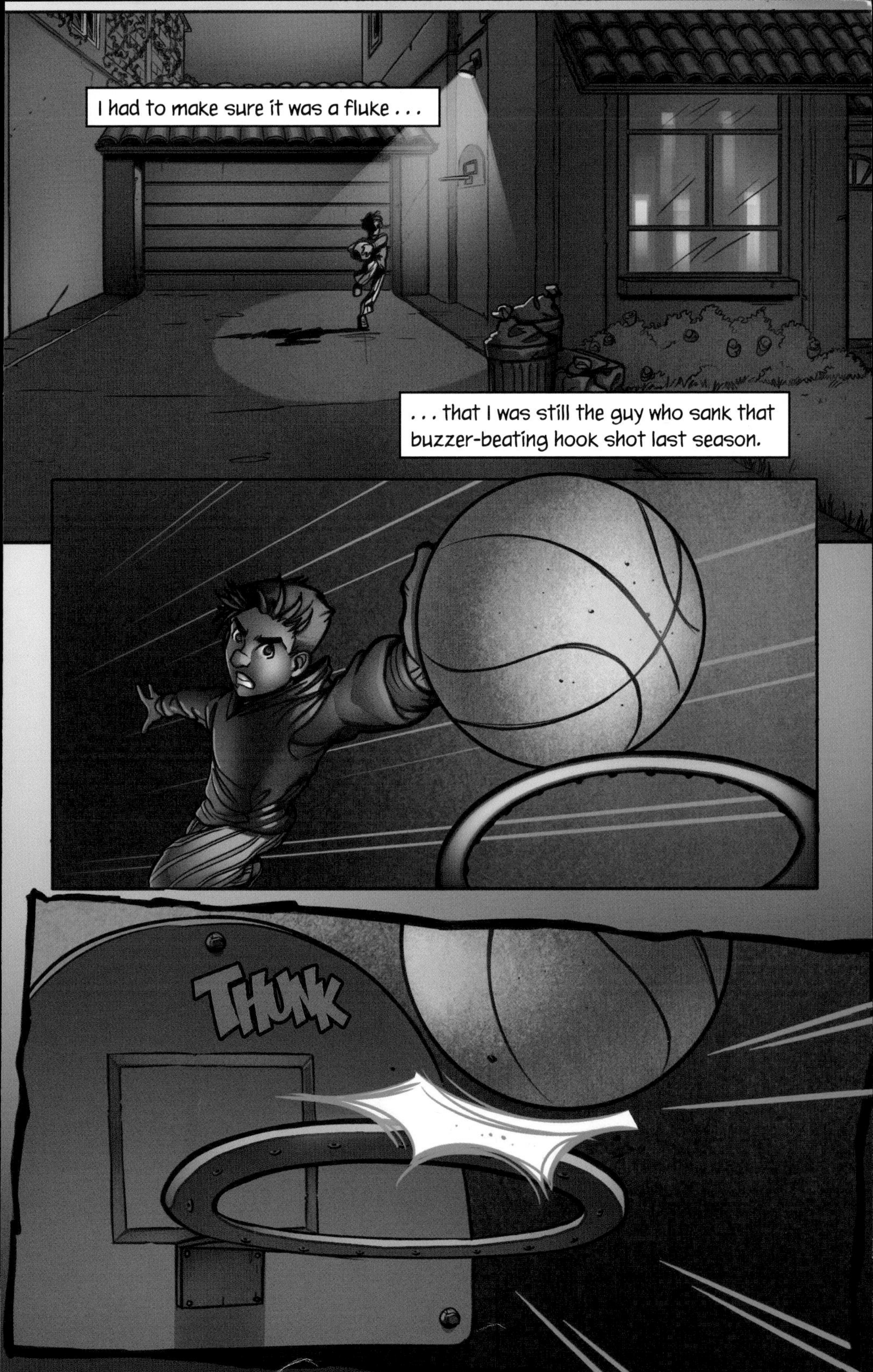

I had to make sure it was a fluke . . .
. . . that I was still the guy who sank that buzzer-beating hook shot last season.
THUNK

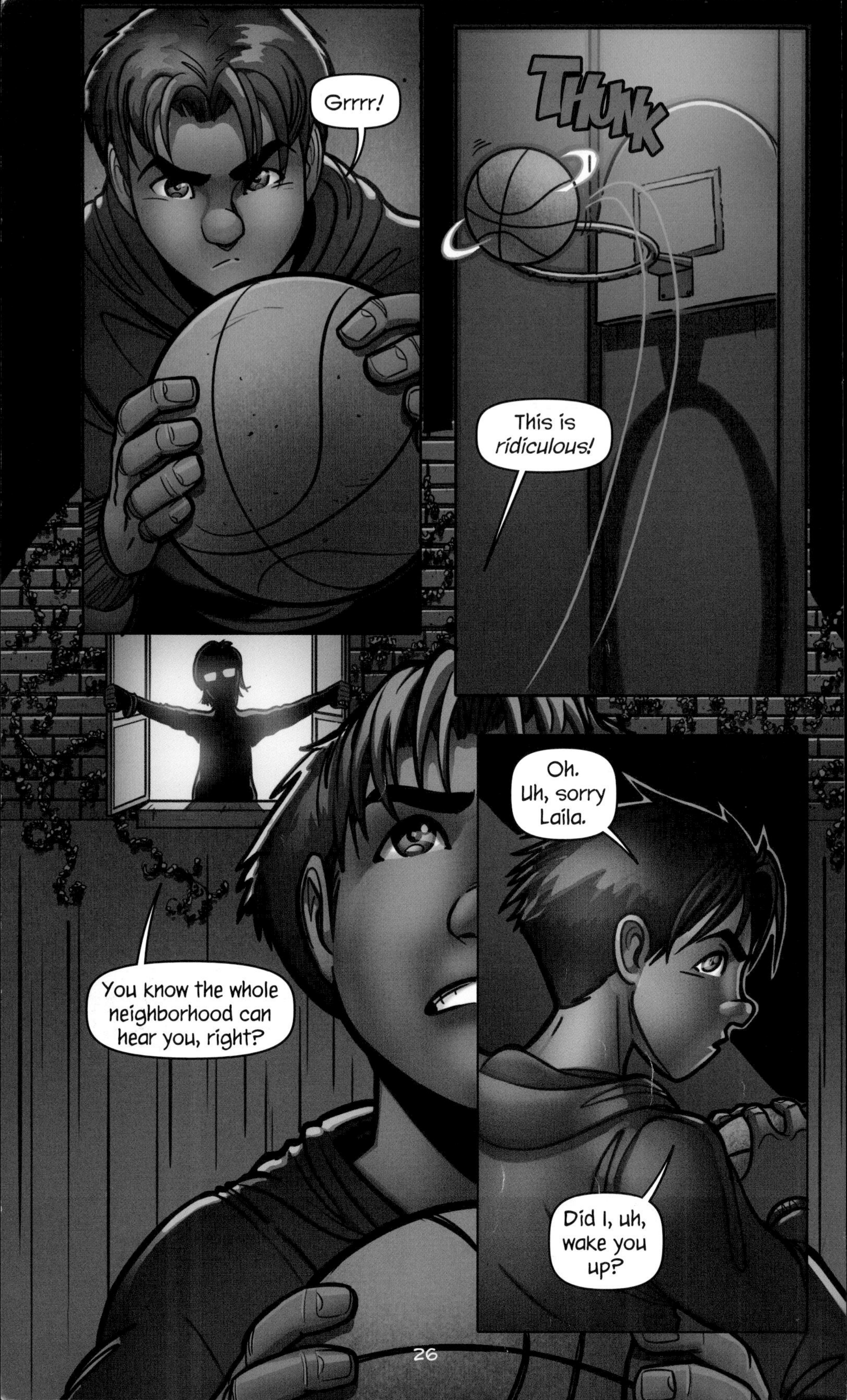

Grrrr!
THUNK
This is ridiculous!
You know the whole neighborhood can hear you, right?
Oh. Uh, sorry Laila.
Did I, uh, wake you up?

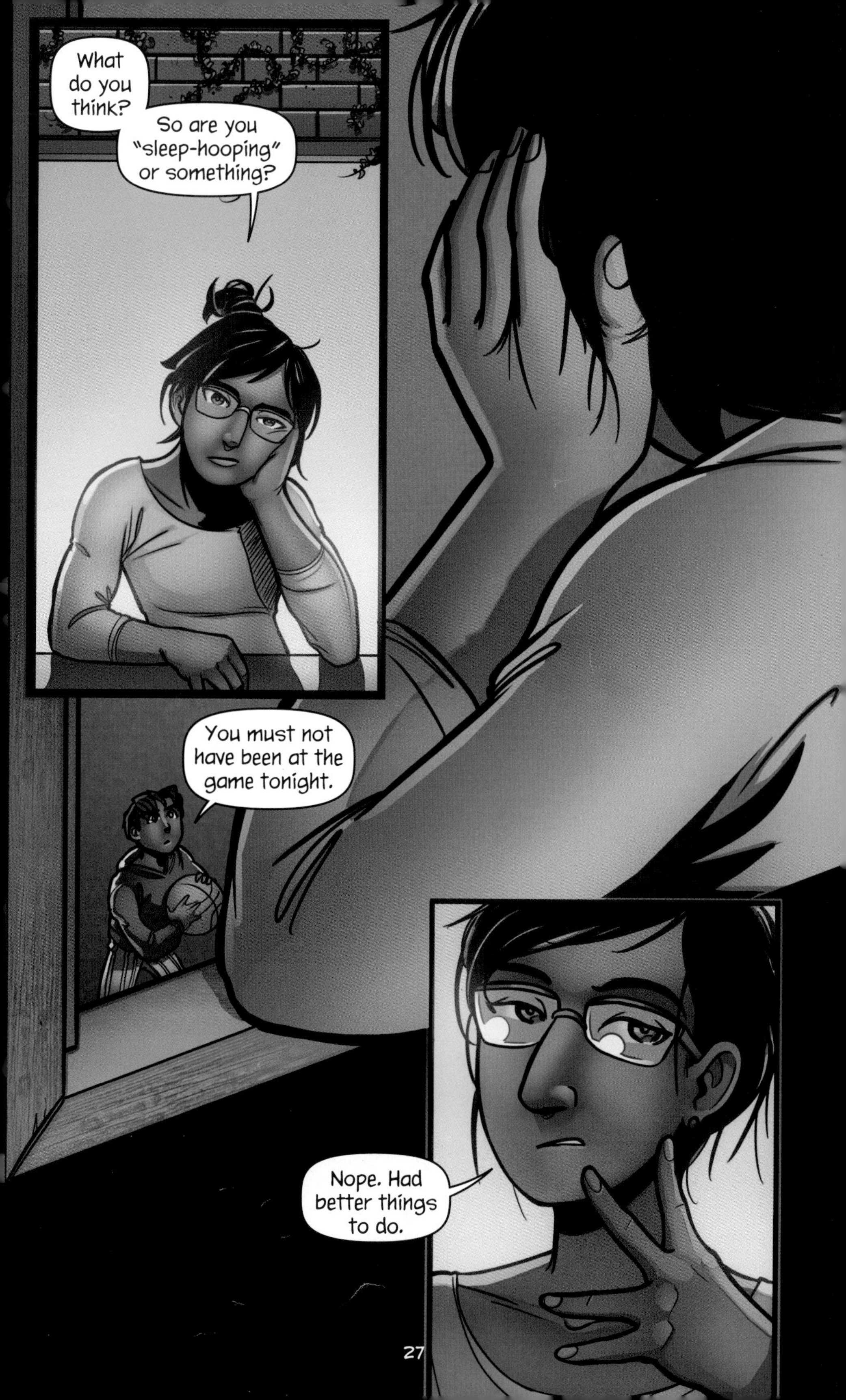
What do you think?
So are you "sleep-hooping" or something?
You must not have been at the game tonight.
Nope. Had better things to do.

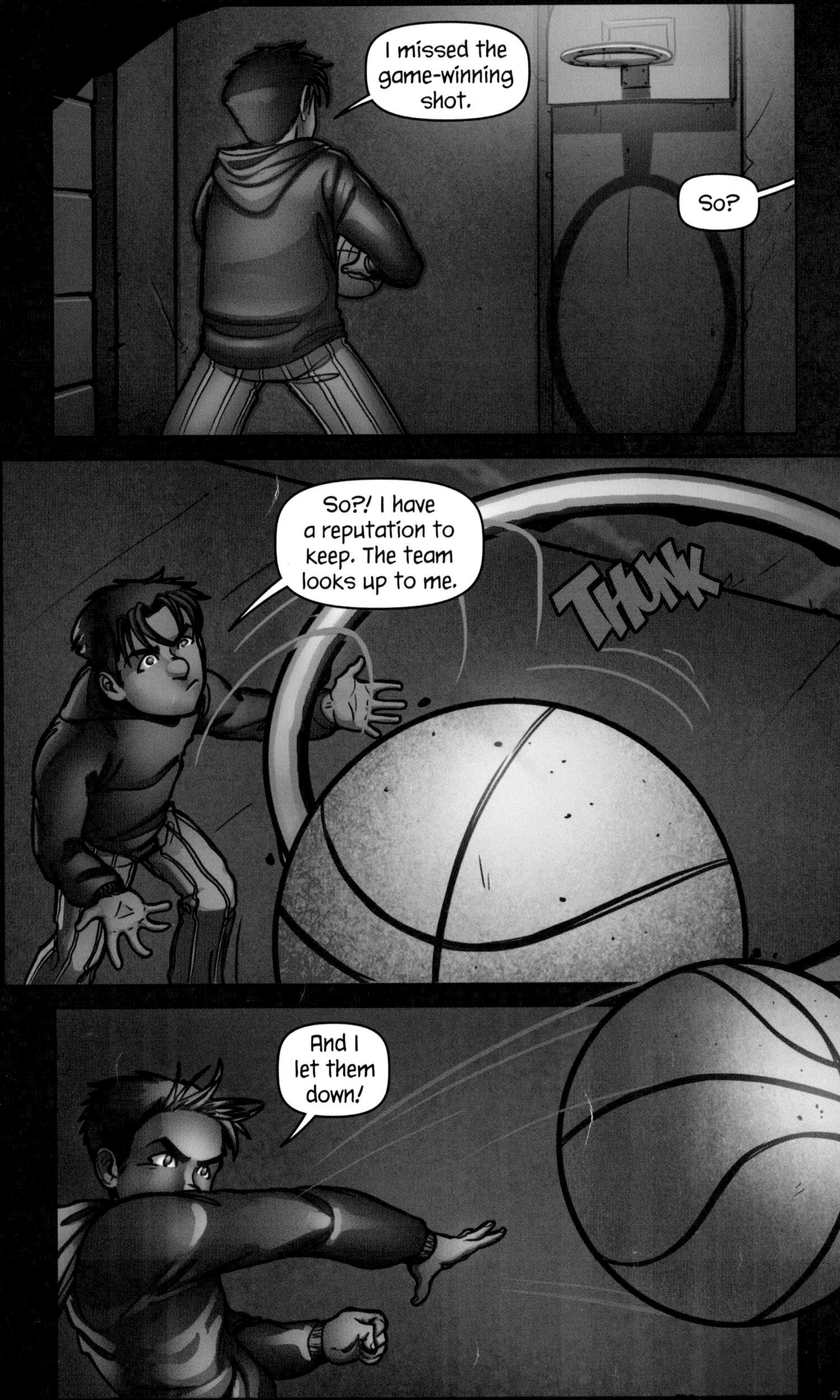
I missed the game-winning shot.
So?
So?! I have a reputation to keep. The team looks up to me.
THUNK
And I let them down!

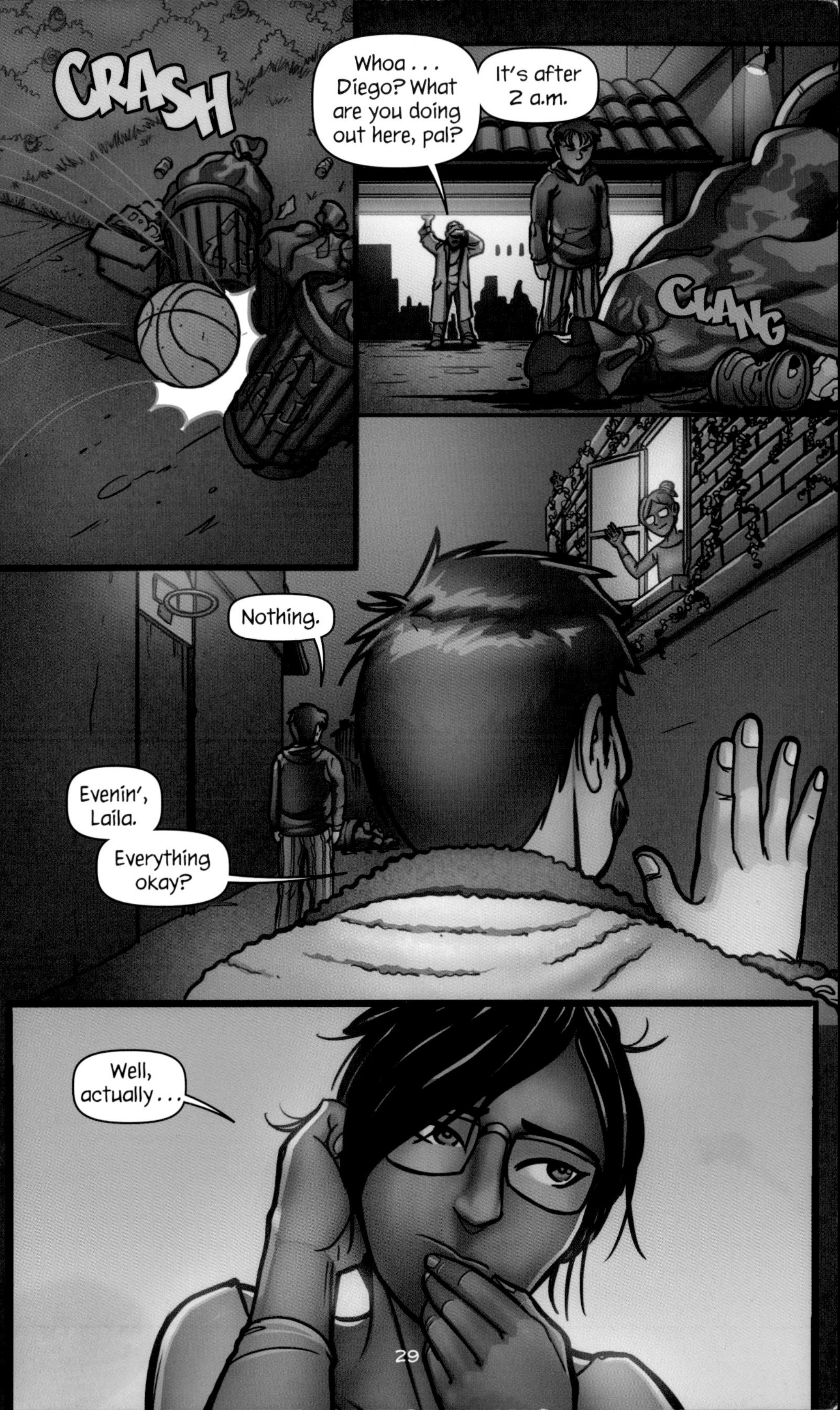
CRASH
Whoa . . . Diego? What are you doing out here, pal?
It's after 2 a.m.
CLANG
Nothing.
Evenin', Laila.
Everything okay?
Well, actually . . .

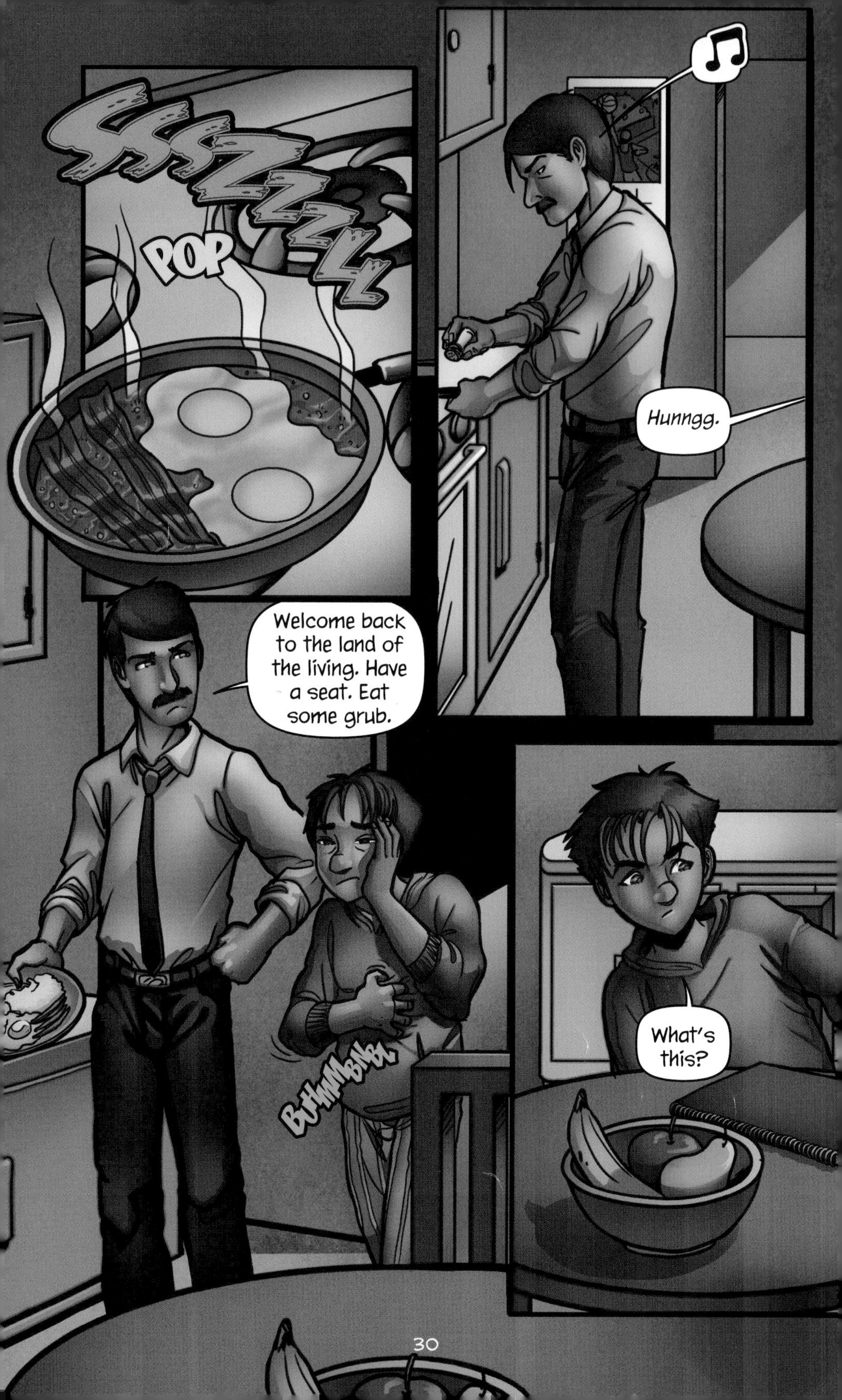
POP
Hunngg.
Welcome back to the land of the living. Have a seat. Eat some grub.
What's this?

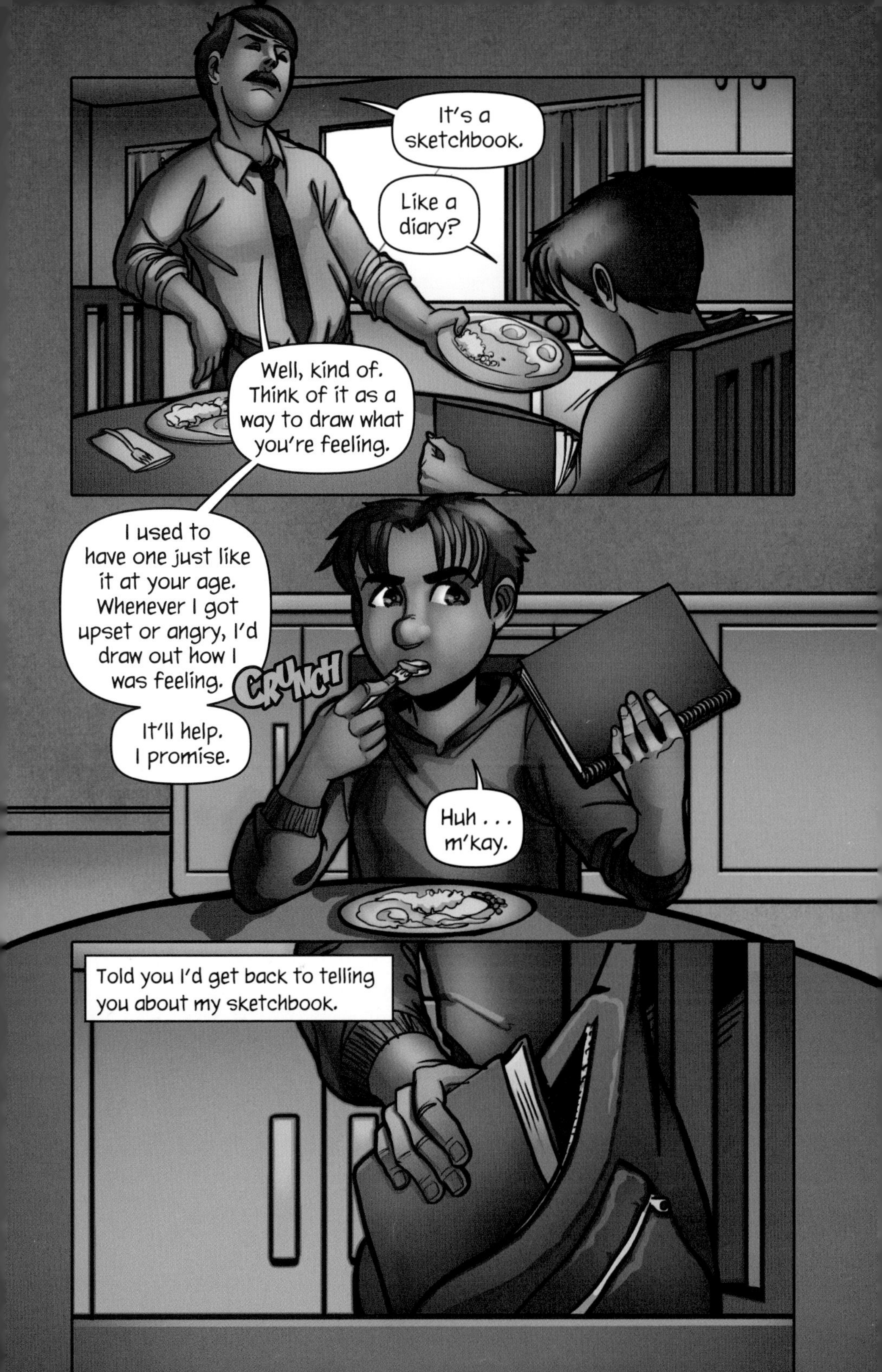
It's a sketchbook.
Like a diary?
Well, kind of. Think of it as a way to draw what you're feeling.
I used to have one just like it at your age. Whenever I got upset or angry, I'd draw out how I was feeling.
It'll help. I promise.
CRUNCH
Huh . . . m'kay.
Told you I'd get back to telling you about my sketchbook.

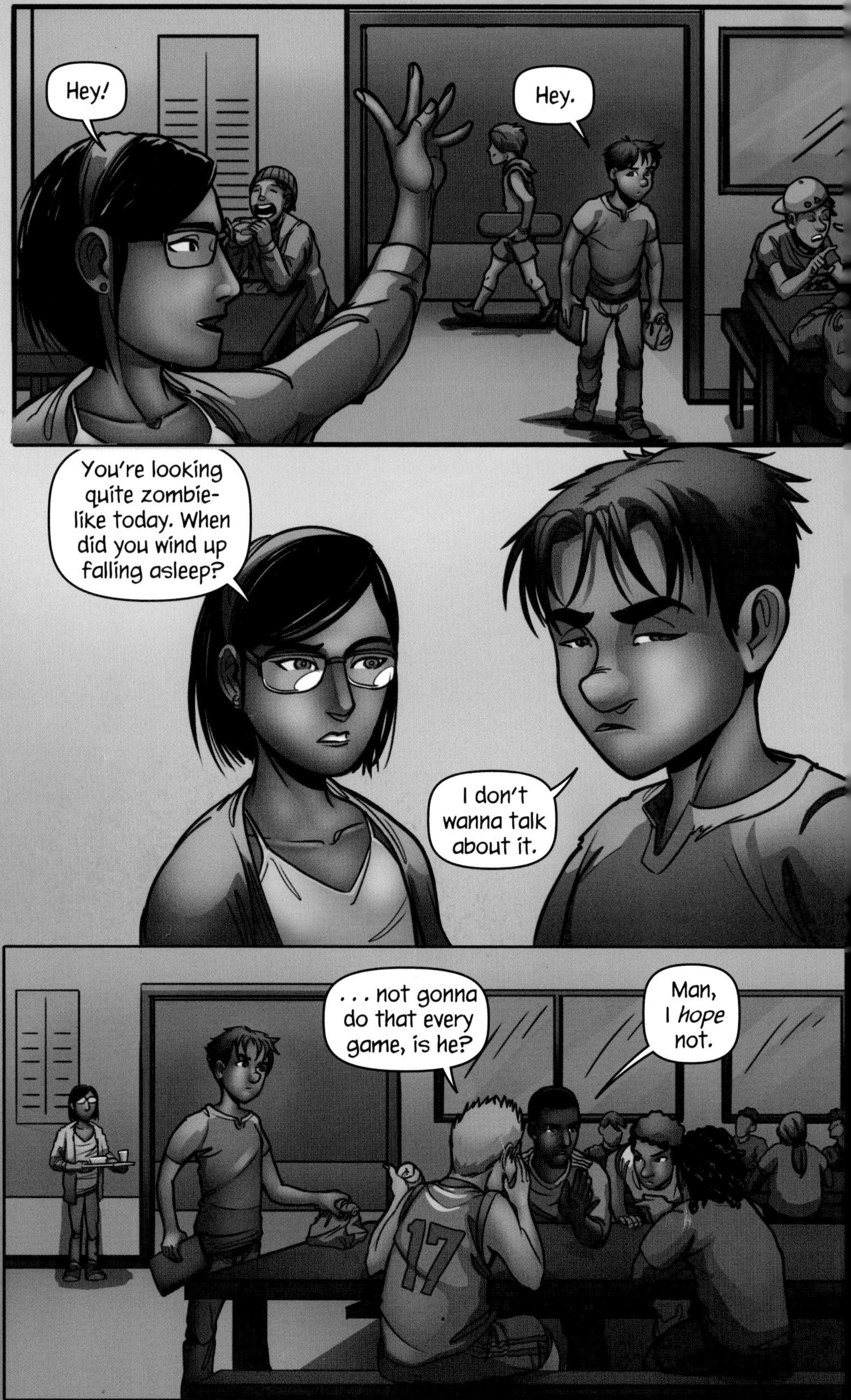
Hey!
Hey.
You're looking quite zombie-like today. When did you wind up falling asleep?
I don't wanna talk about it.
. . . not gonna do that every game, is he?
Man, I *hope* not.

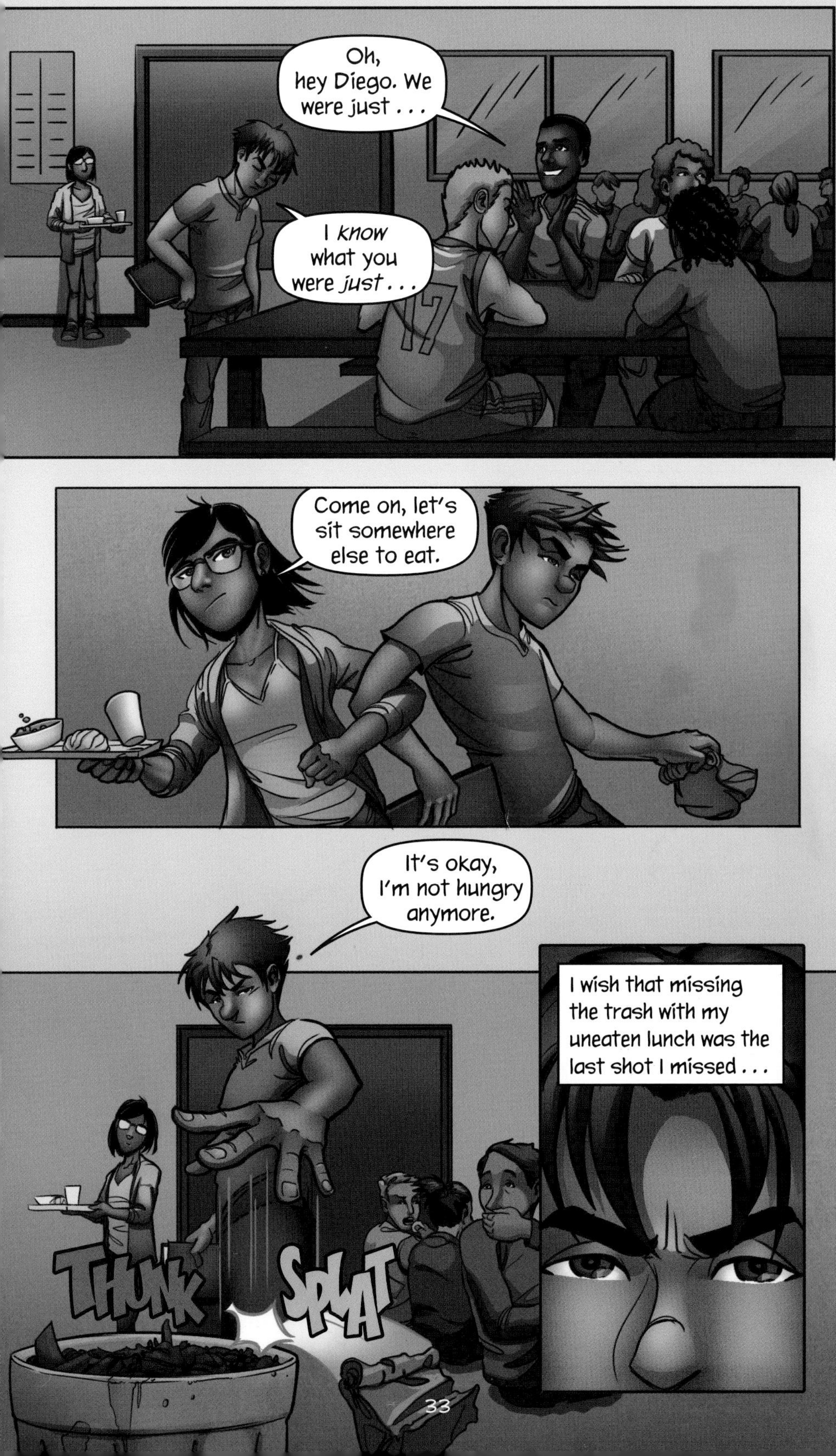
Oh, hey Diego. We were just . . .
I *know* what you were *just* . . .
Come on, let's sit somewhere else to eat.
It's okay, I'm not hungry anymore.
THUNK
SPLAT
I wish that missing the trash with my uneaten lunch was the last shot I missed . . .

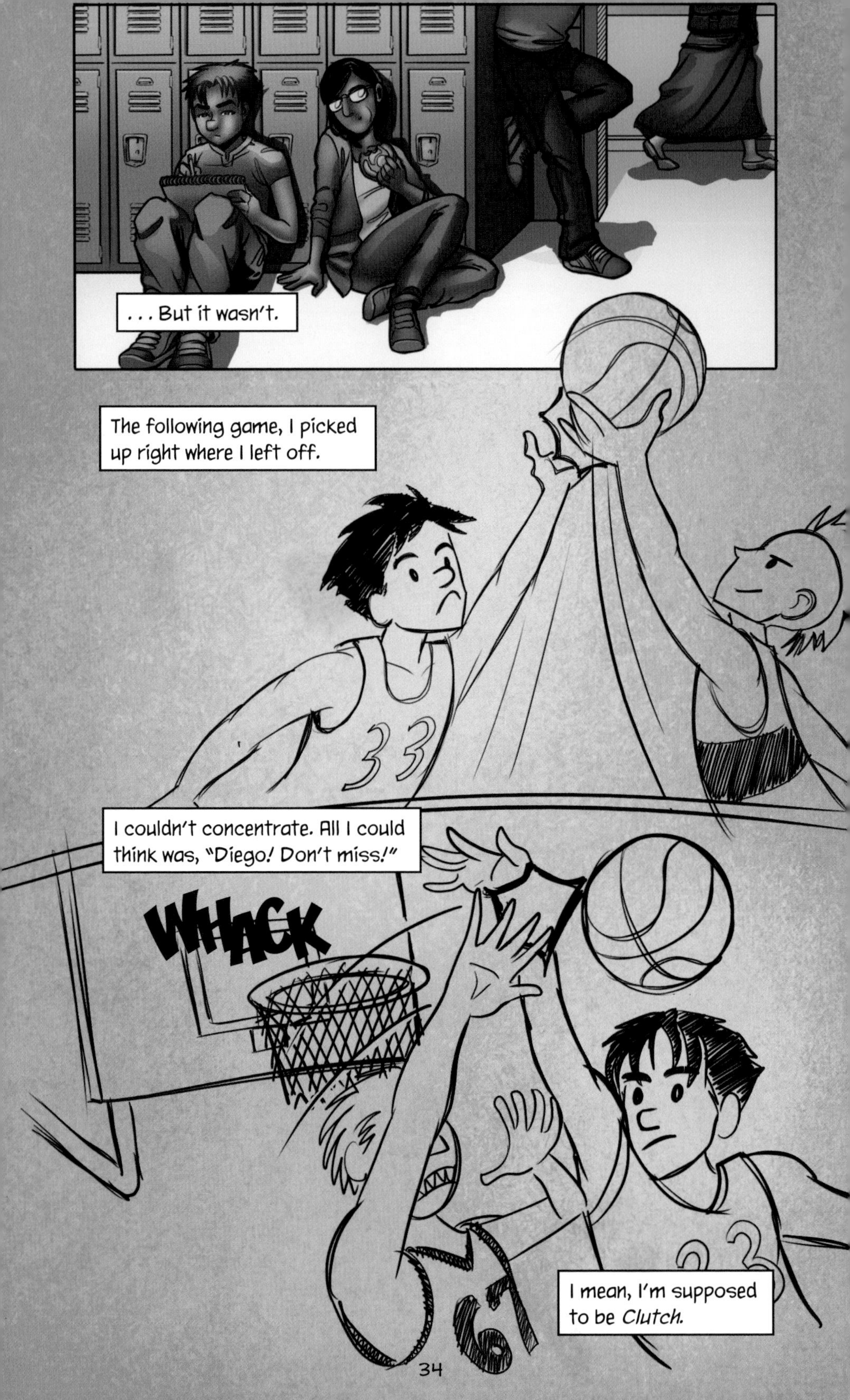
. . . But it wasn't.
The following game, I picked up right where I left off.
33
I couldn't concentrate. All I could think was, "Diego! Don't miss!"
WHACK
33
I mean, I'm supposed to be *Clutch.*

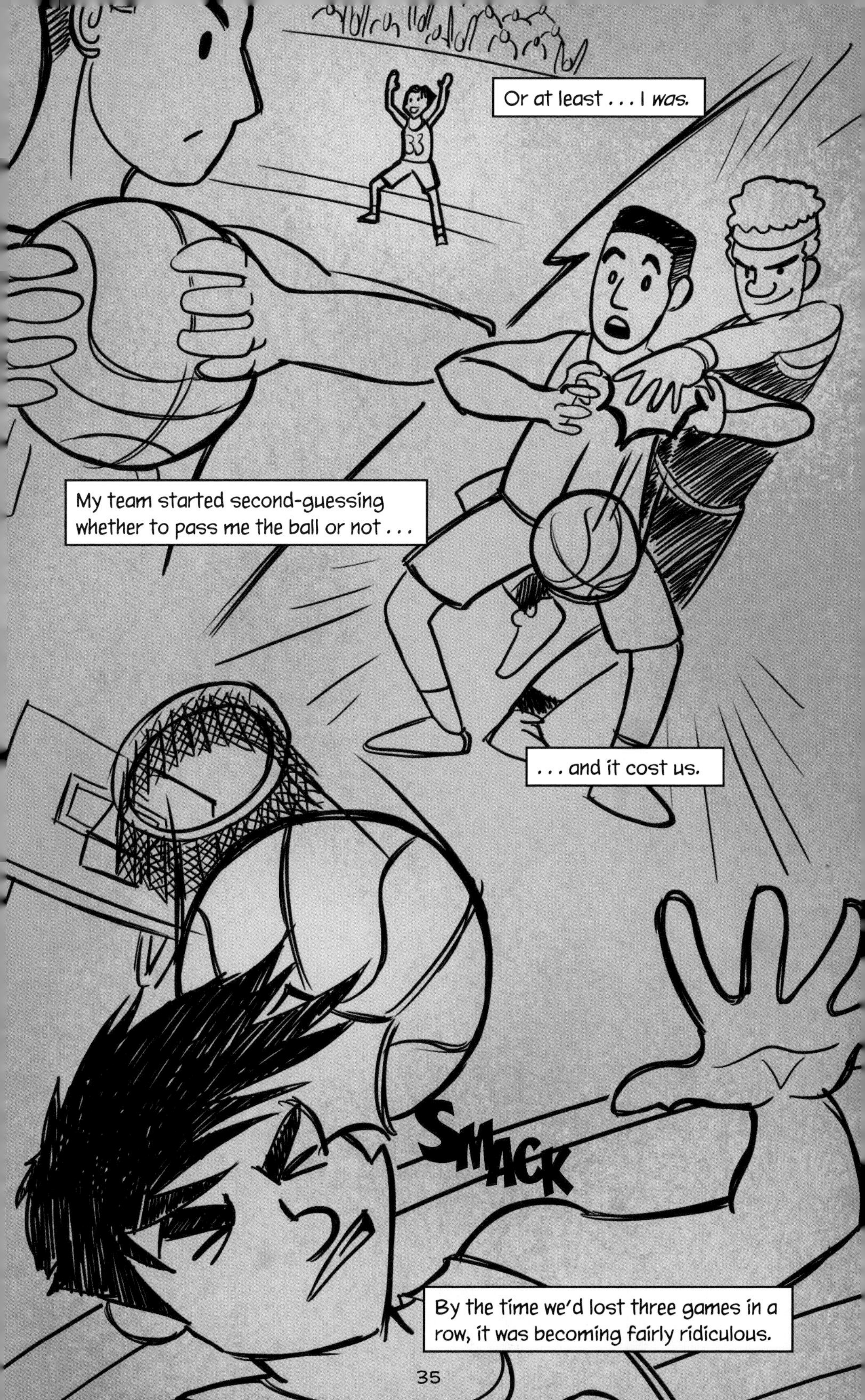
Or at least . . . I *was.*
My team started second-guessing whether to pass me the ball or not . . .
. . . and it cost us.
SMACK
By the time we'd lost three games in a row, it was becoming fairly ridiculous.

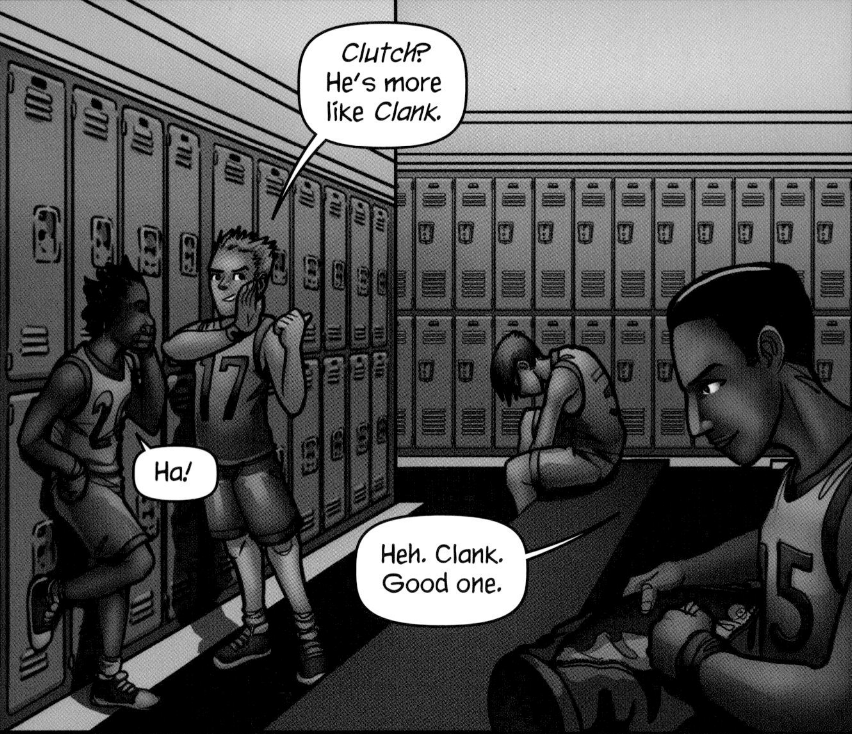
Clutch? He's more like *Clank.*
Ha!
Heh. Clank. Good one.

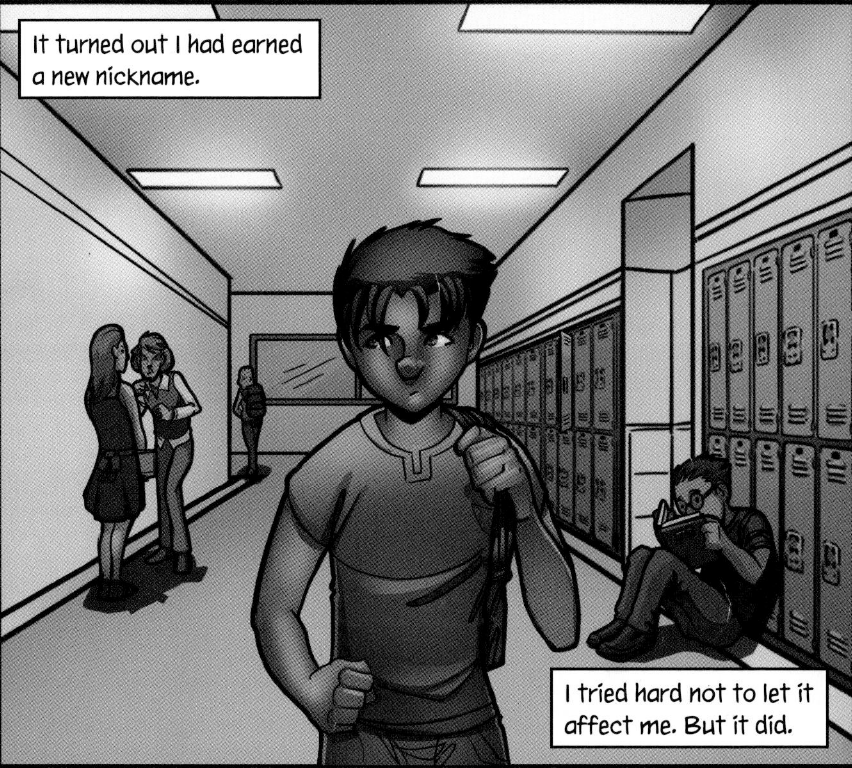
It turned out I had earned a new nickname.
I tried hard not to let it affect me. But it did.

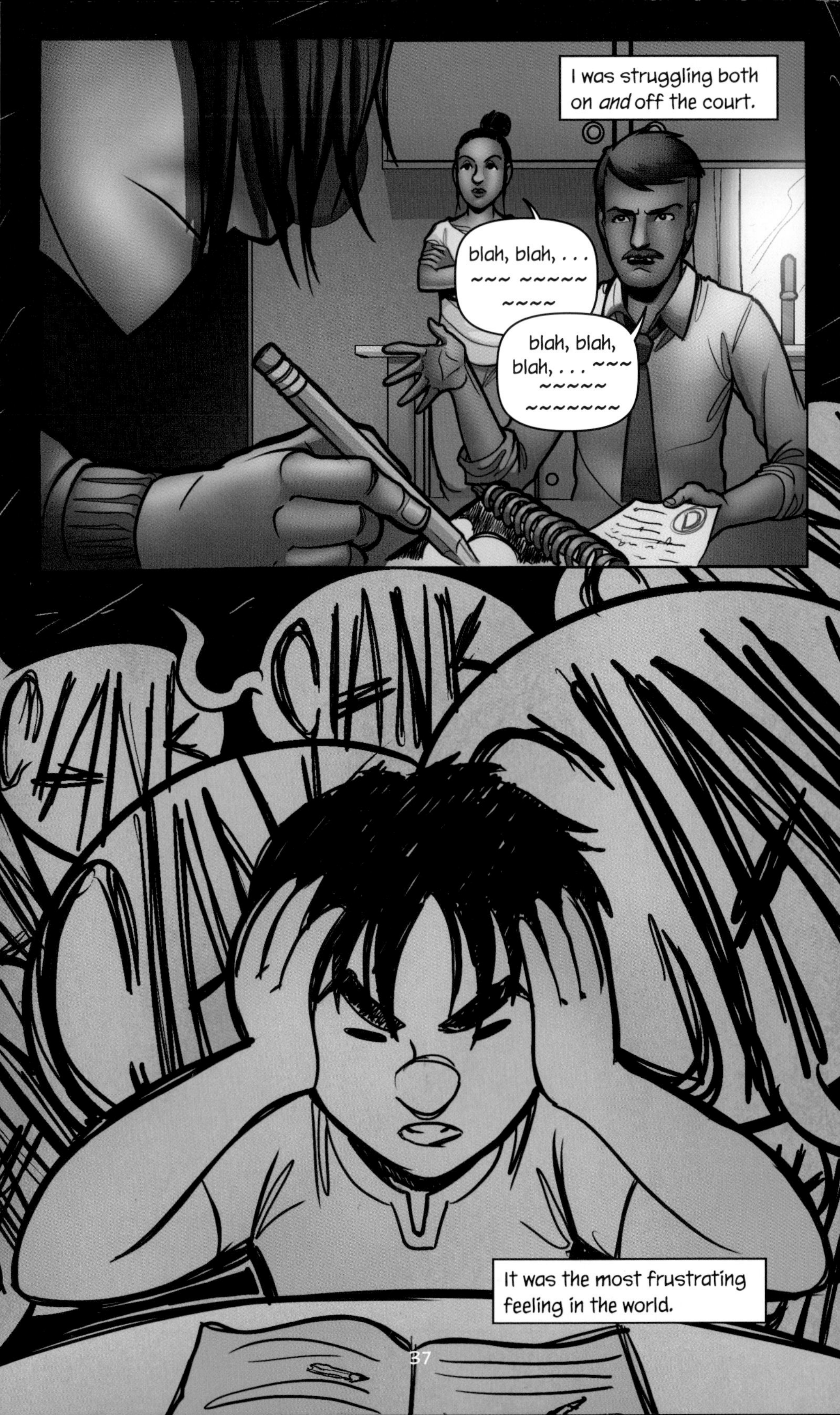
I was struggling both on *and* off the court.
blah, blah, . . . ~~~ ~~~~~ ~~~~
blah, blah, blah, . . . ~~~ ~~~~~ ~~~~~~~
CLANK CLANK
It was the most frustrating feeling in the world.

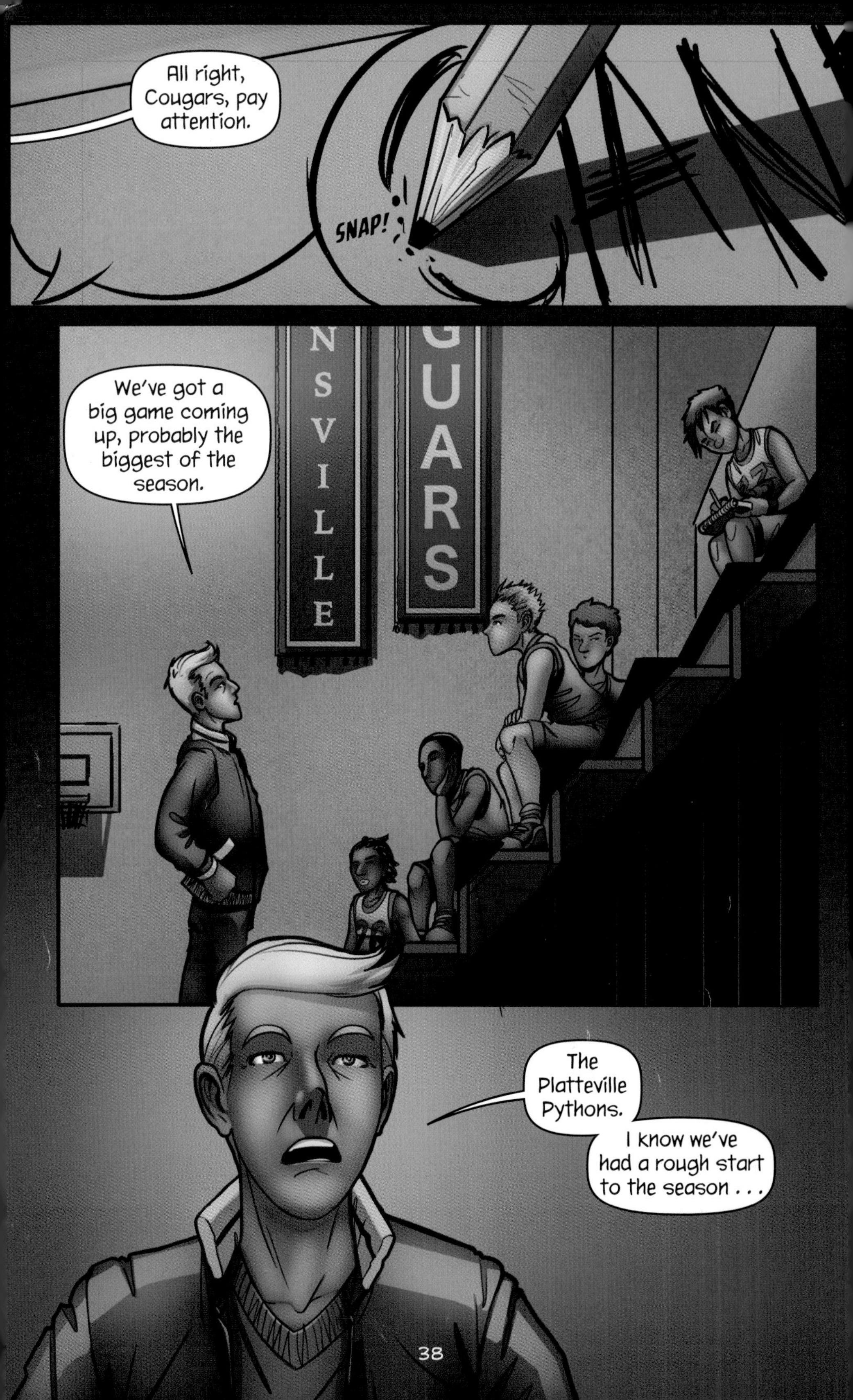
All right, Cougars, pay attention.
SNAP!
NSVILLE
GUARS
We've got a big game coming up, probably the biggest of the season.
The Platteville Pythons.
I know we've had a rough start to the season . . .

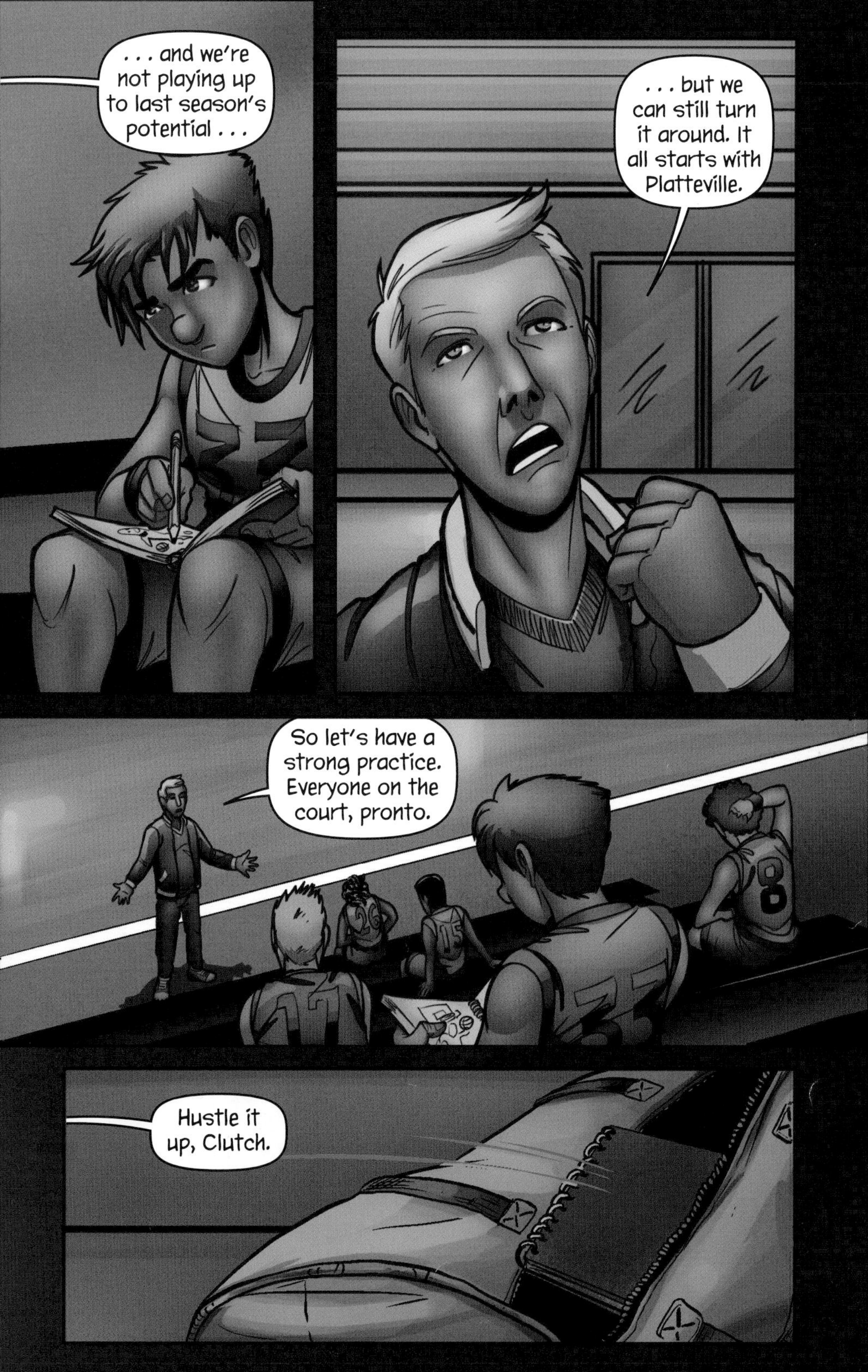
. . . and we're not playing up to last season's potential . . .
. . . but we can still turn it around. It all starts with Platteville.
So let's have a strong practice. Everyone on the court, pronto.
Hustle it up, Clutch.

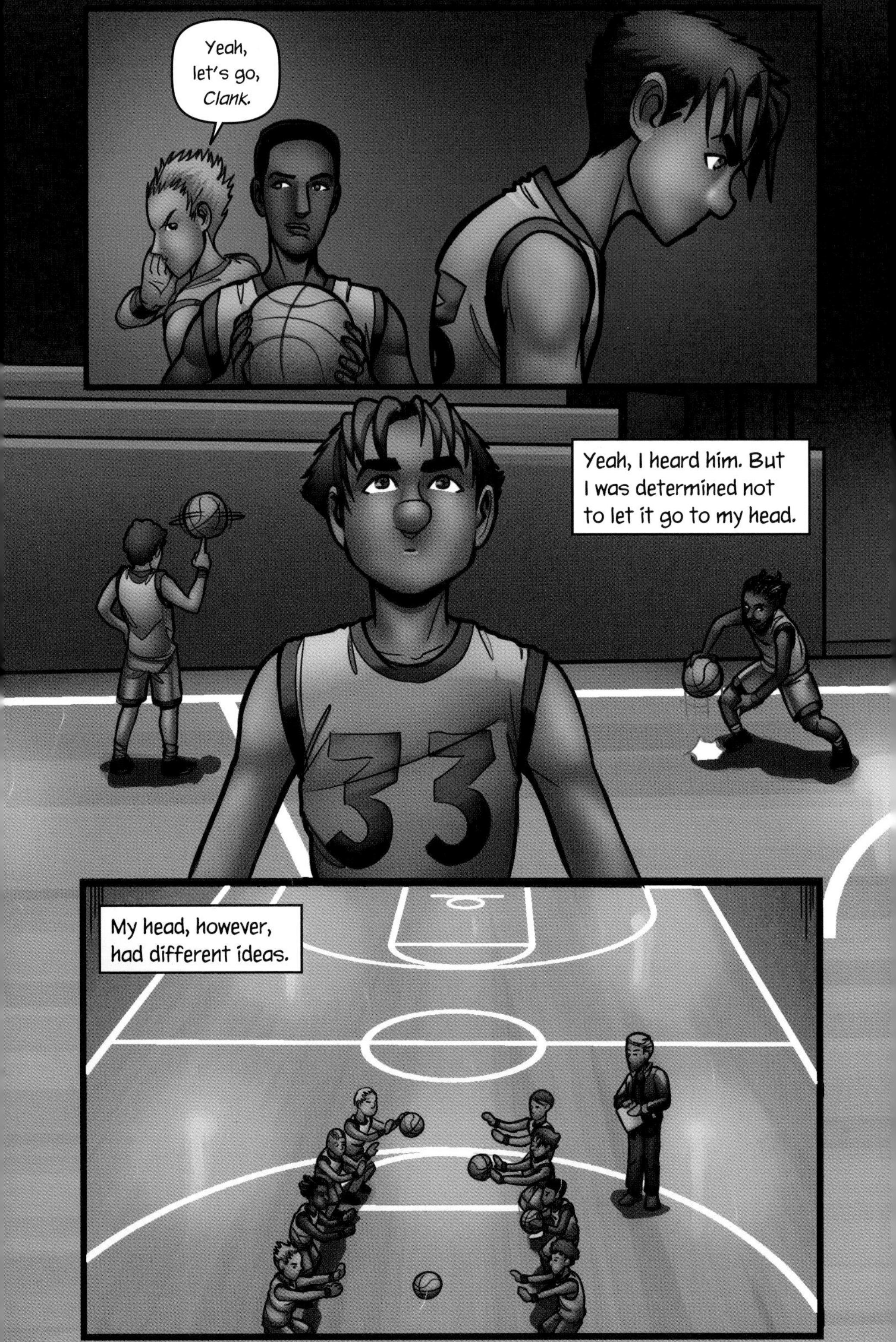
Yeah, let's go, *Clank.*
Yeah, I heard him. But I was determined not to let it go to my head.
My head, however, had different ideas.

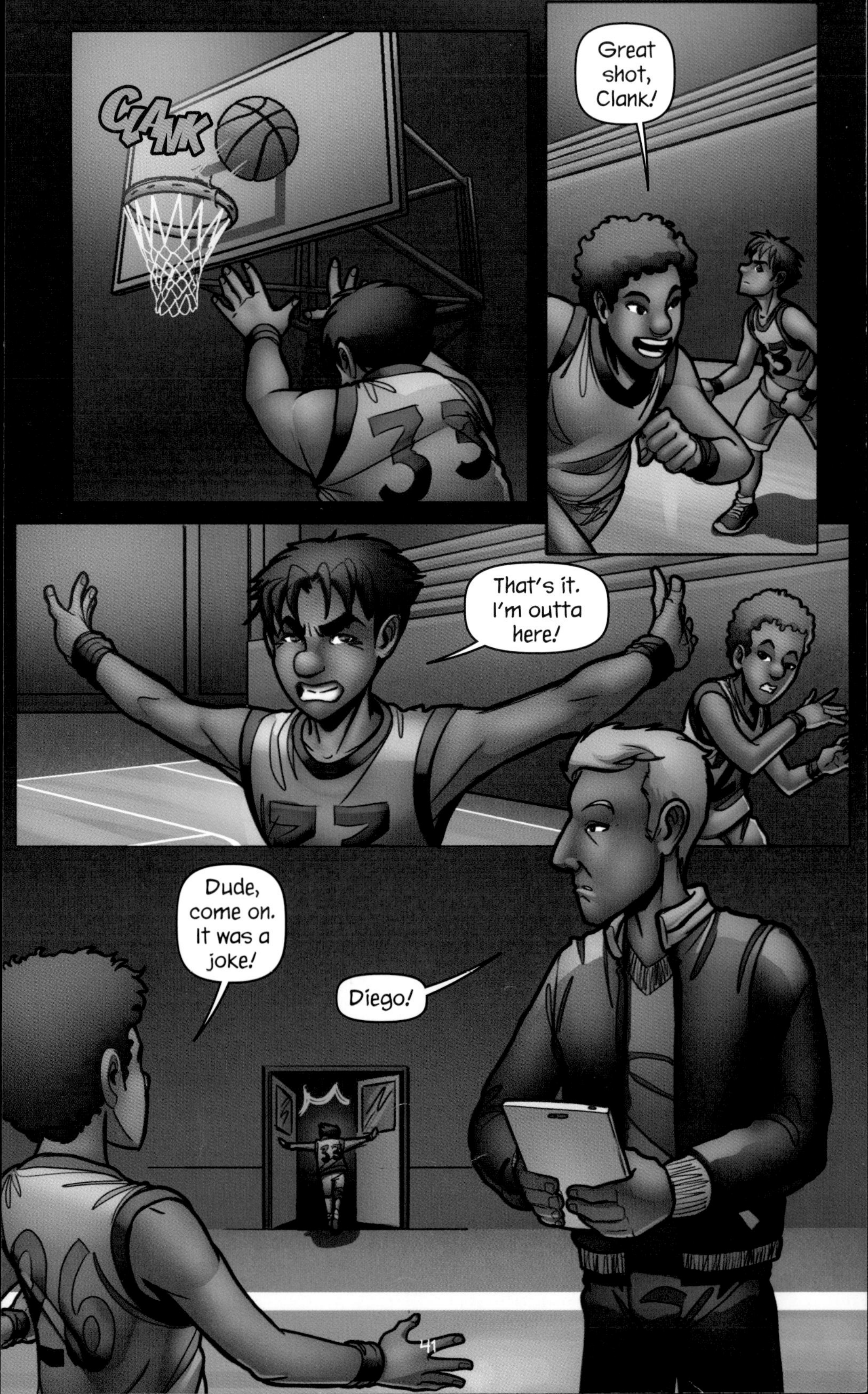
CLANK
Great shot, Clank!
That's it. I'm outta here!
Dude, come on. It was a joke!
Diego!

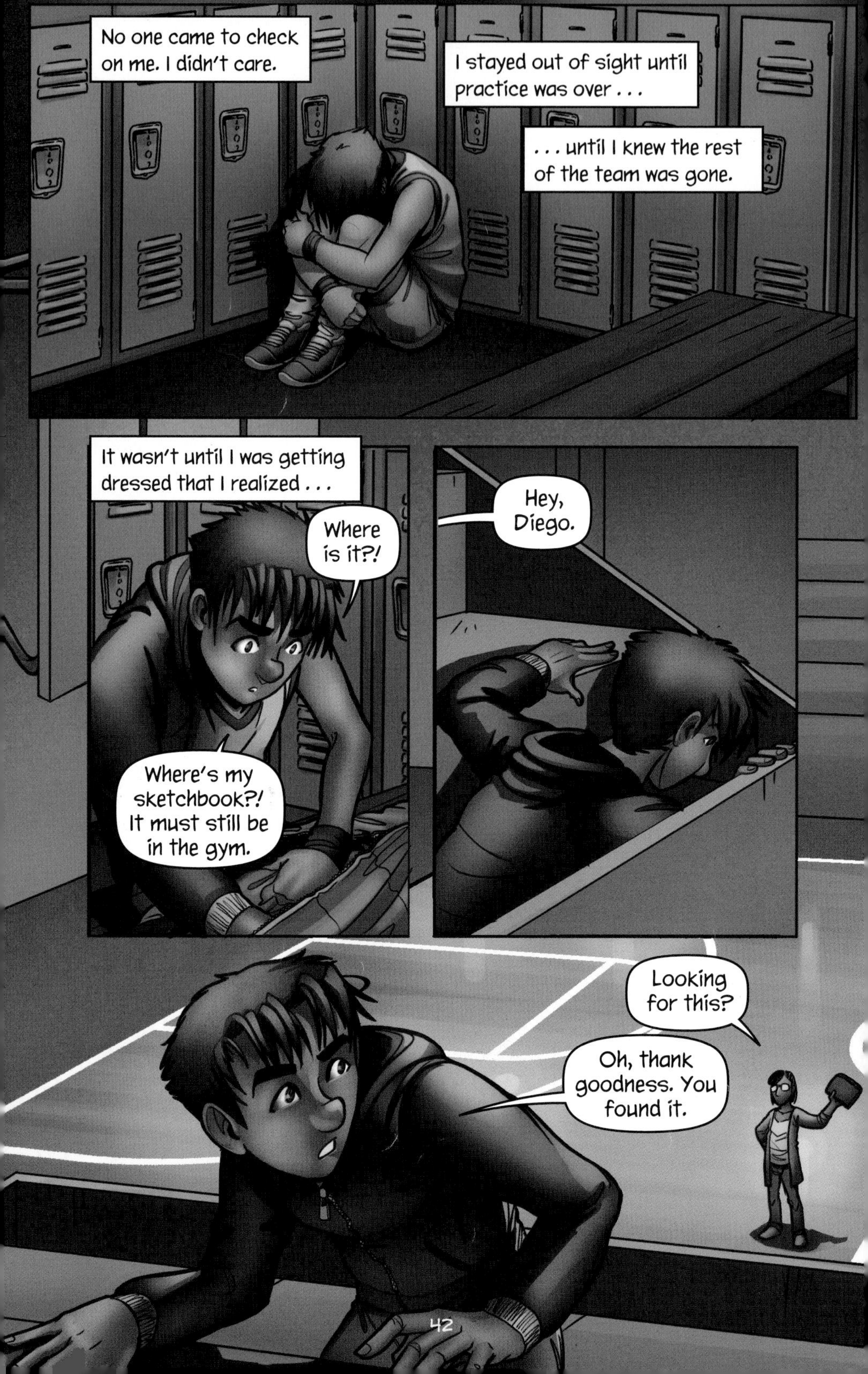
No one came to check on me. I didn't care.
I stayed out of sight until practice was over . . .
. . . until I knew the rest of the team was gone.
It wasn't until I was getting dressed that I realized . . .
Where is it?!
Where's my sketchbook?! It must still be in the gym.
Hey, Diego.
Looking for this?
Oh, thank goodness. You found it.

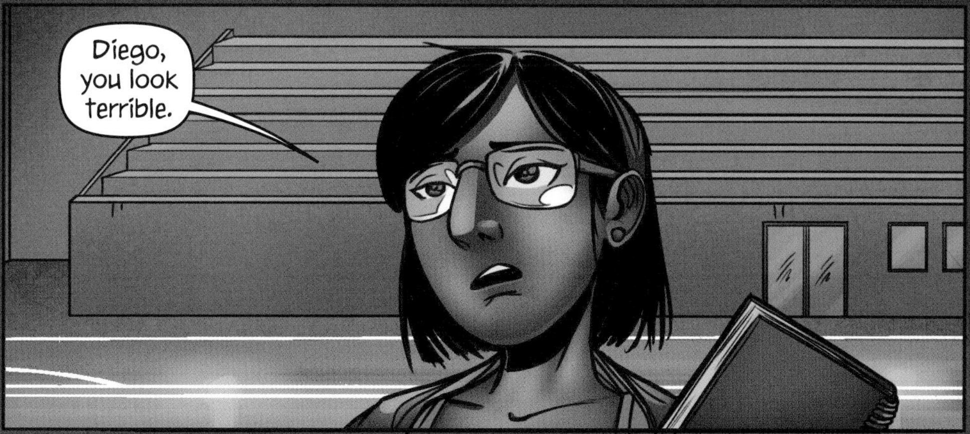
Diego, you look terrible.

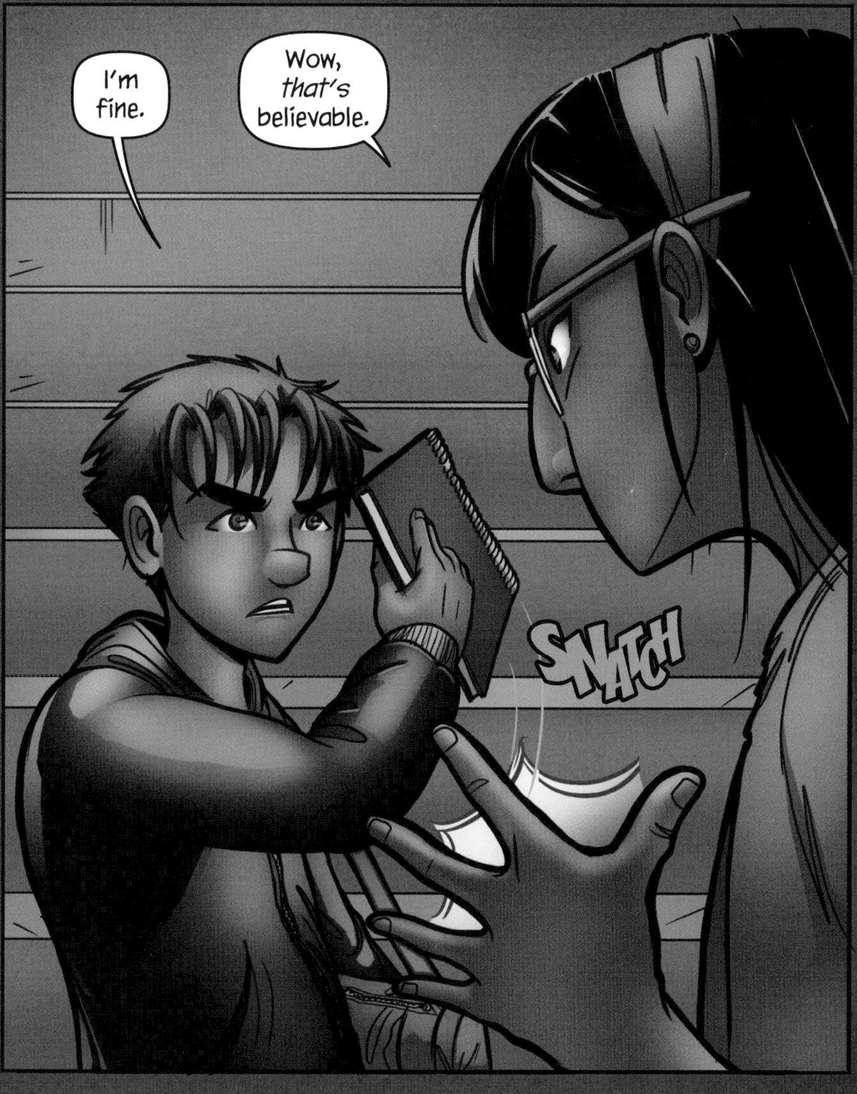
I'm fine.
Wow, *that's* believable.
SNATCH

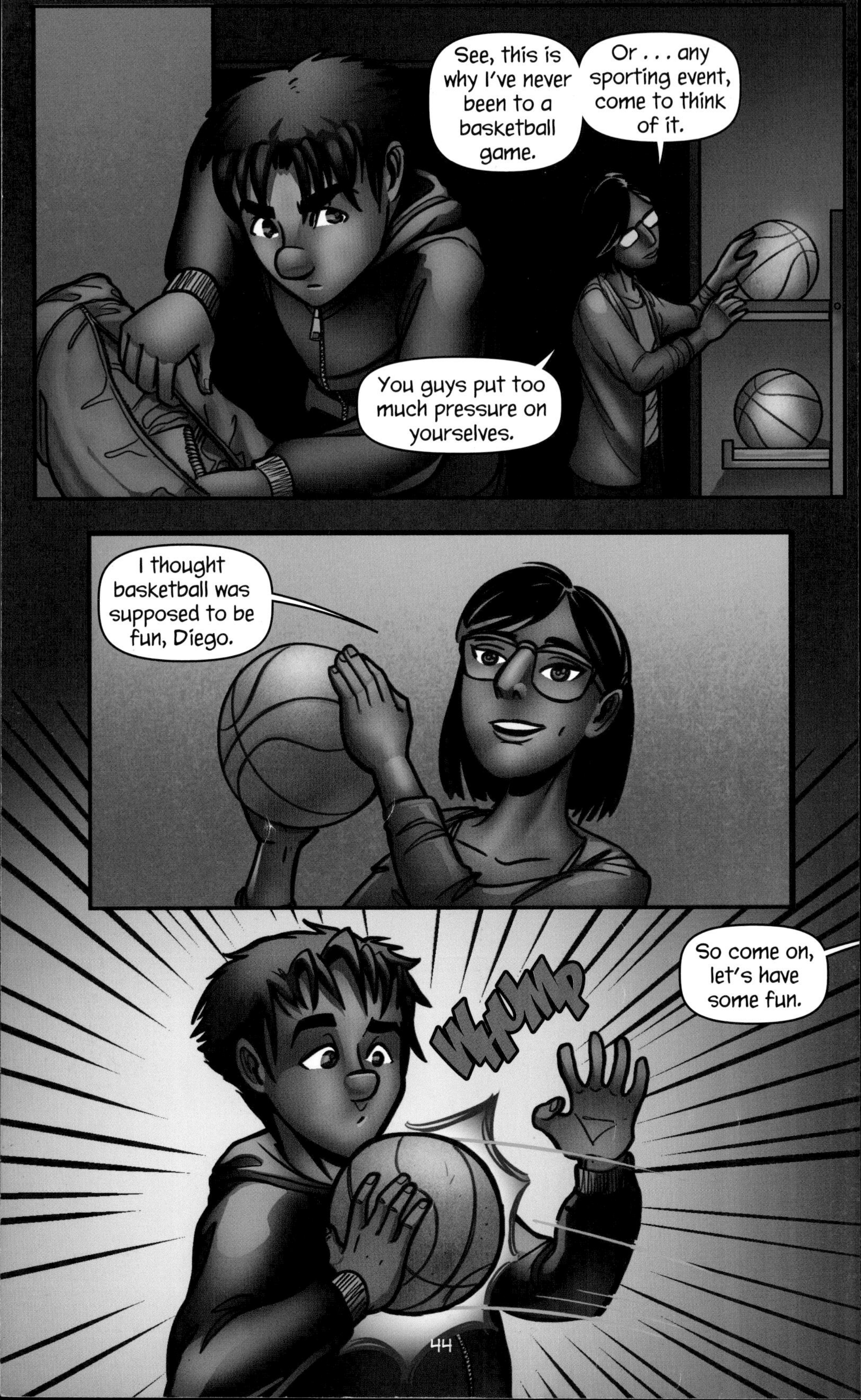

See, this is why I've never been to a basketball game.
Or . . . any sporting event, come to think of it.
You guys put too much pressure on yourselves.
I thought basketball was supposed to be fun, Diego.
So come on, let's have some fun.
WHUMP

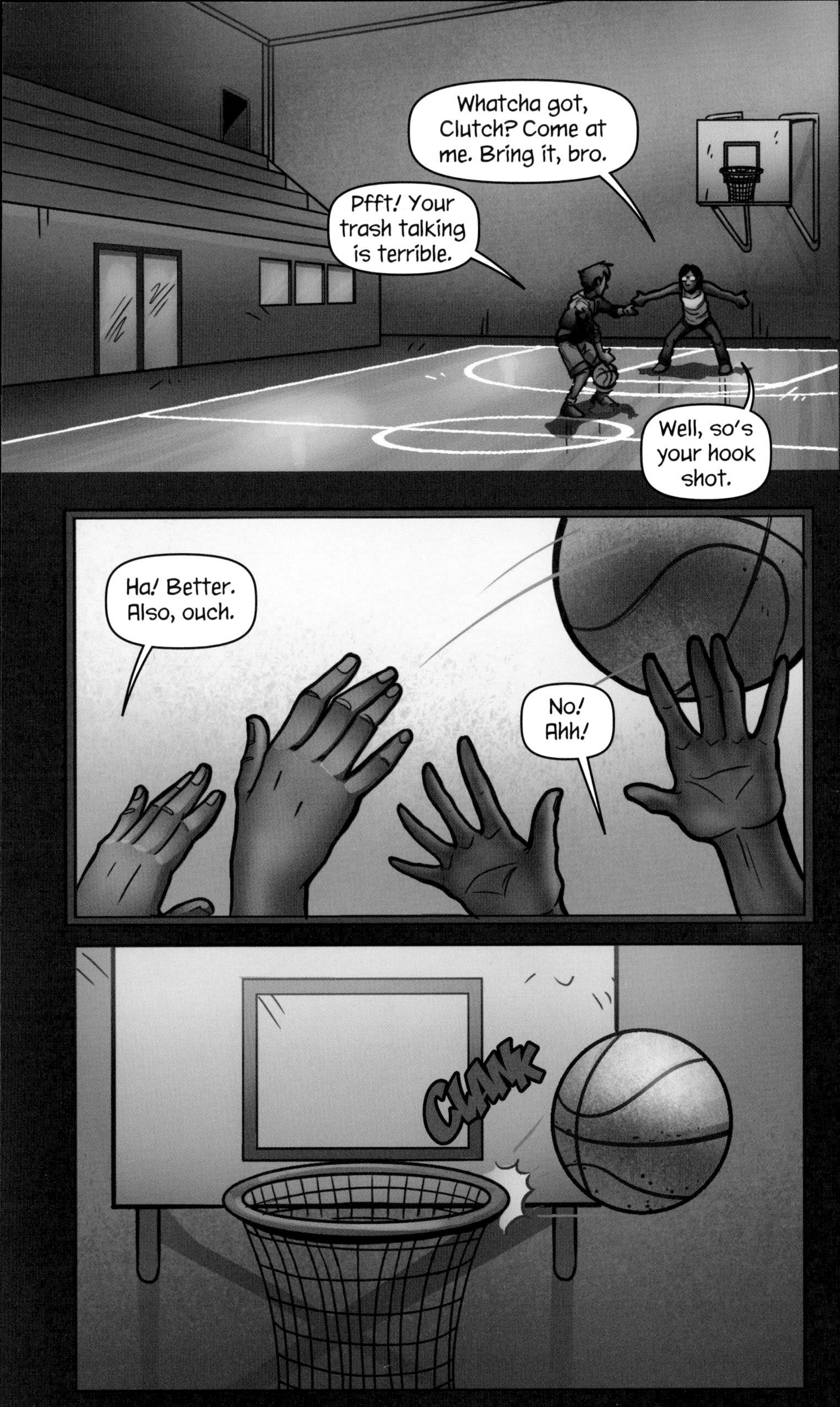
Whatcha got, Clutch? Come at me. Bring it, bro.
Pfft! Your trash talking is terrible.
Well, so's your hook shot.
Ha! Better. Also, ouch.
No! Ahh!
CLANK

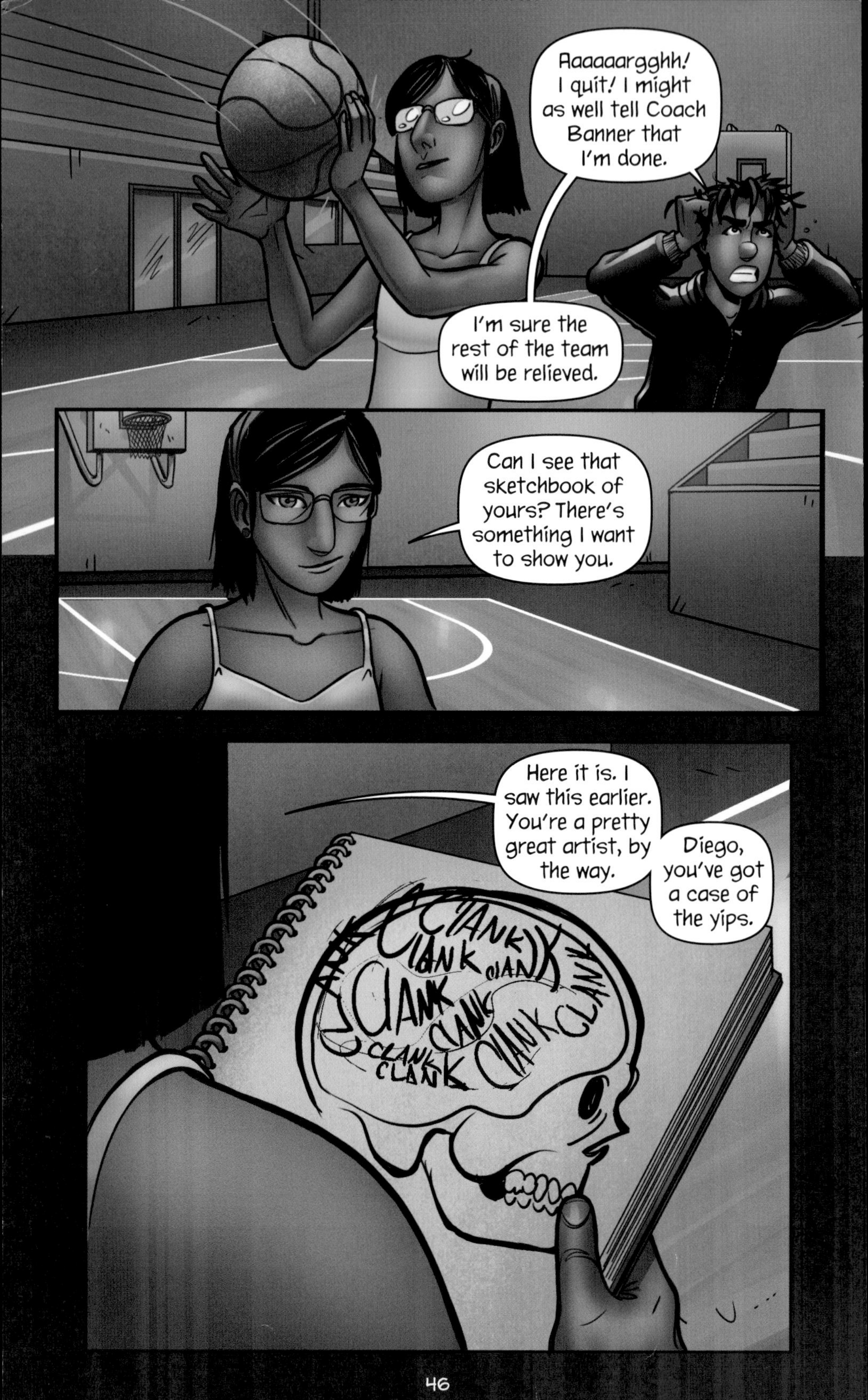
Aaaaaargghh! I quit! I might as well tell Coach Banner that I'm done.
I'm sure the rest of the team will be relieved.
Can I see that sketchbook of yours? There's something I want to show you.
Here it is. I saw this earlier. You're a pretty great artist, by the way.
Diego, you've got a case of the yips.
CLANK CLANK CLANK CLANK CLANK CLANK

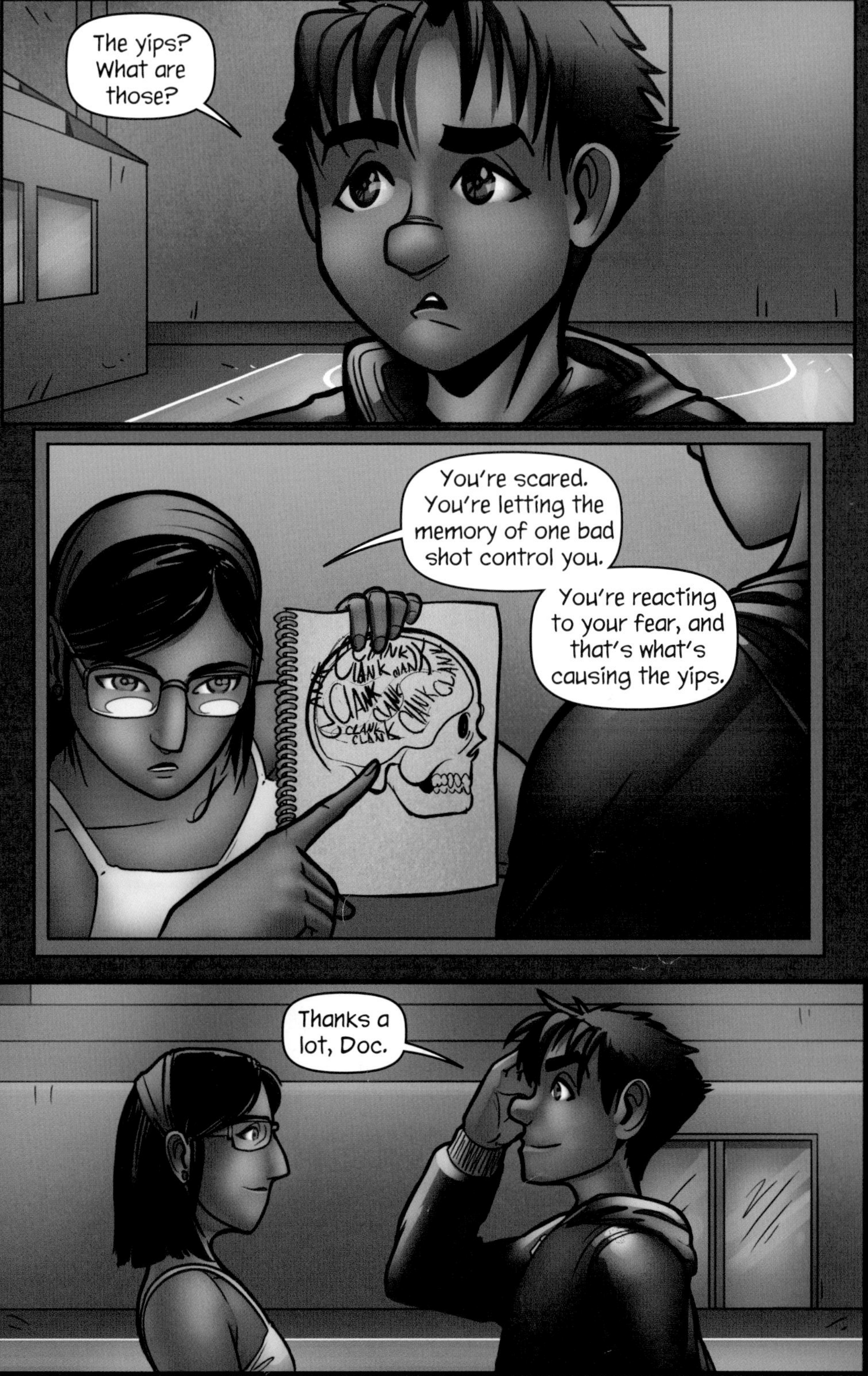
The yips? What are those?
You're scared. You're letting the memory of one bad shot control you.
CLANK CLANK CLANK CLANK CLANK CLANK CLANK
You're reacting to your fear, and that's what's causing the yips.
Thanks a lot, Doc.

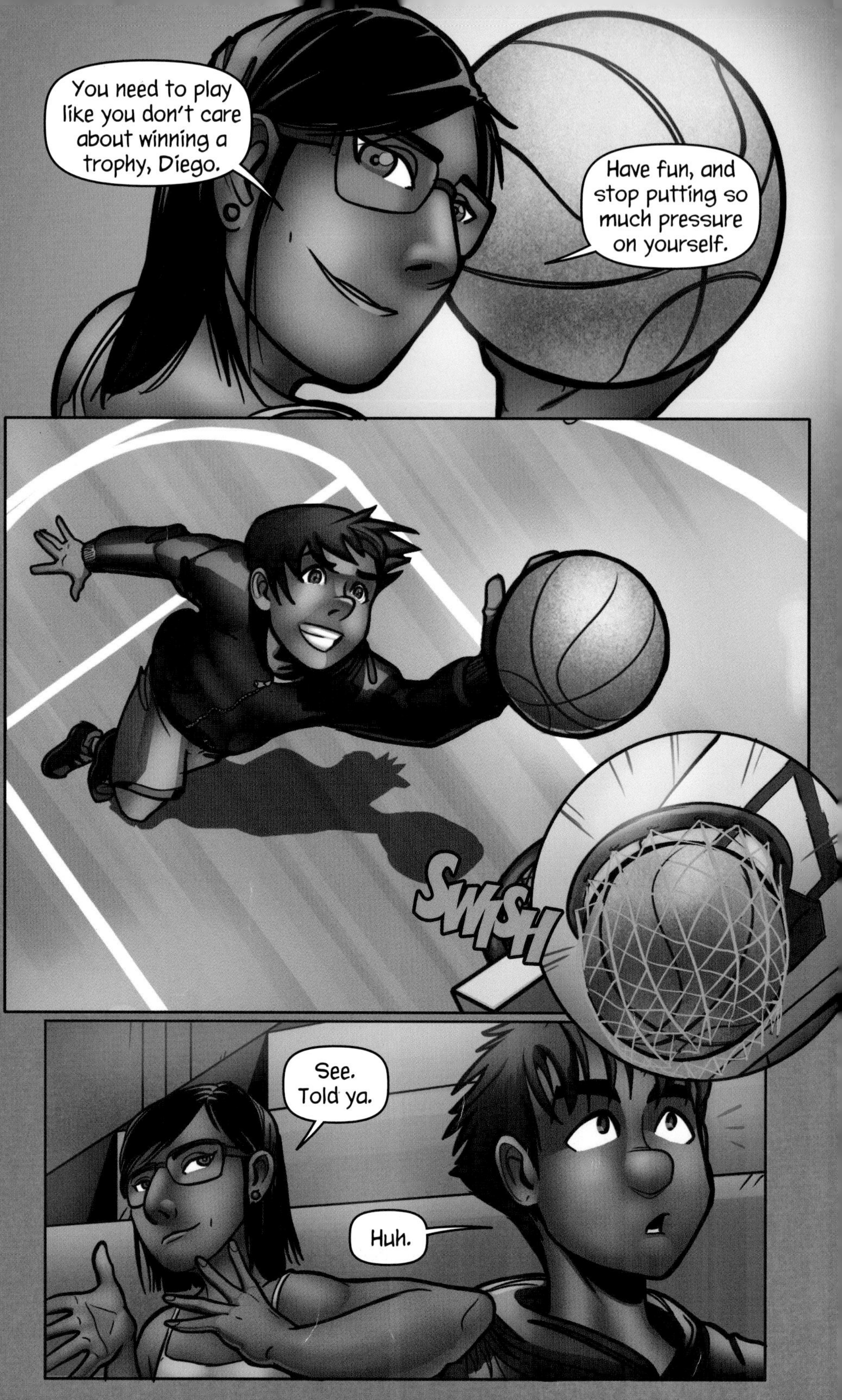
You need to play like you don't care about winning a trophy, Diego.
Have fun, and stop putting so much pressure on yourself.
SWISH
See. Told ya.
Huh.

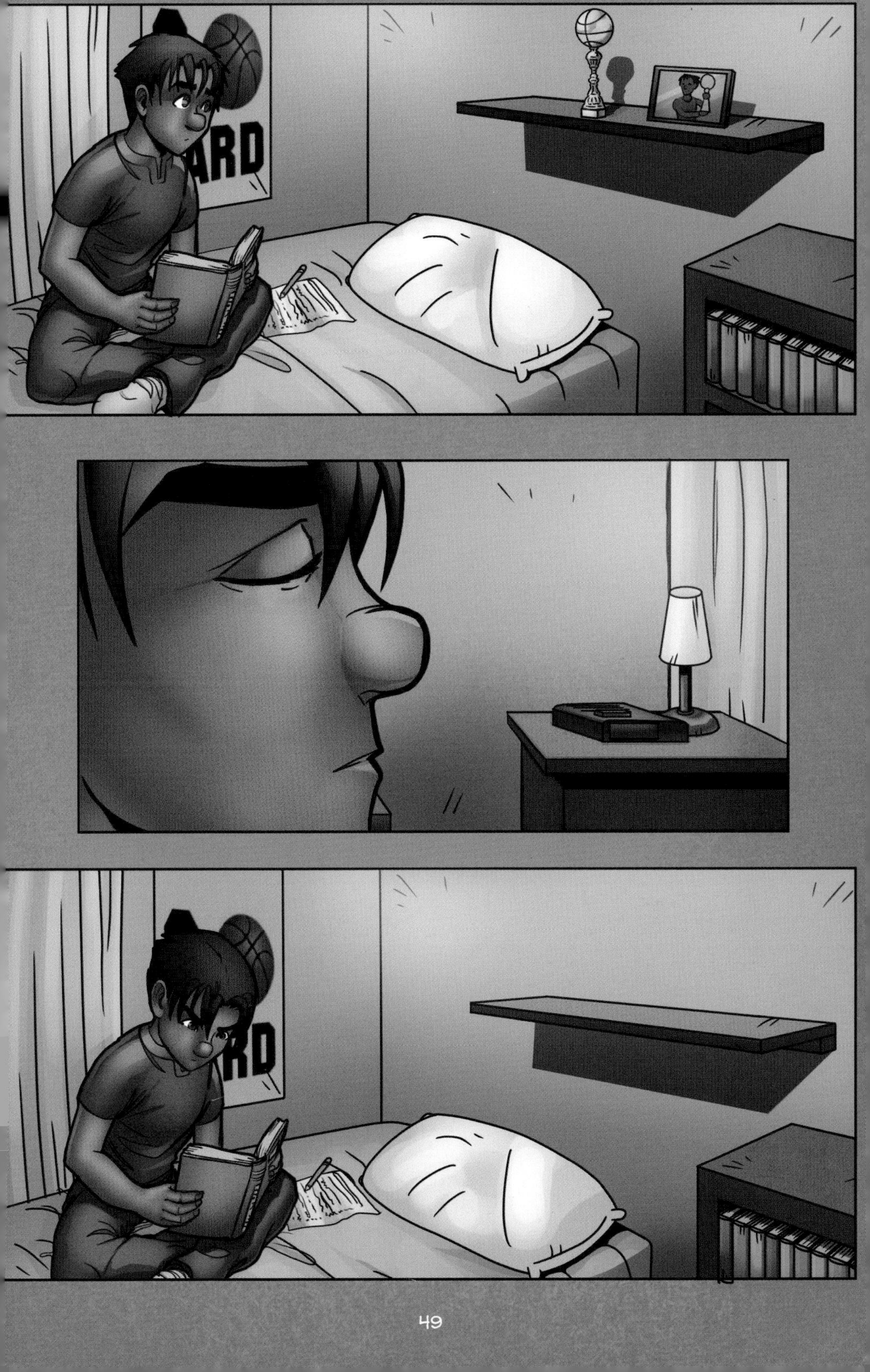
ARD
ARD

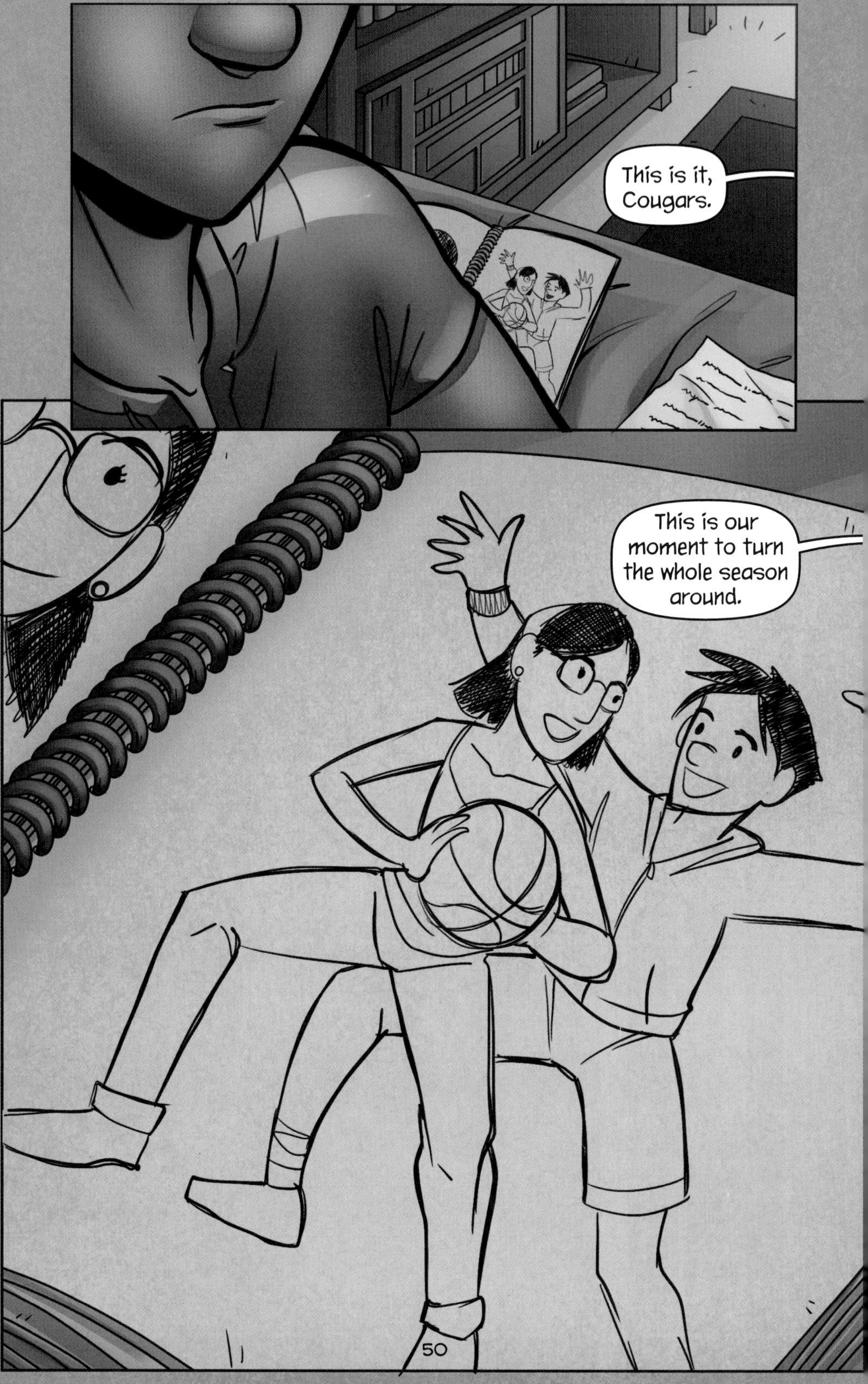
This is it, Cougars.
This is our moment to turn the whole season around.

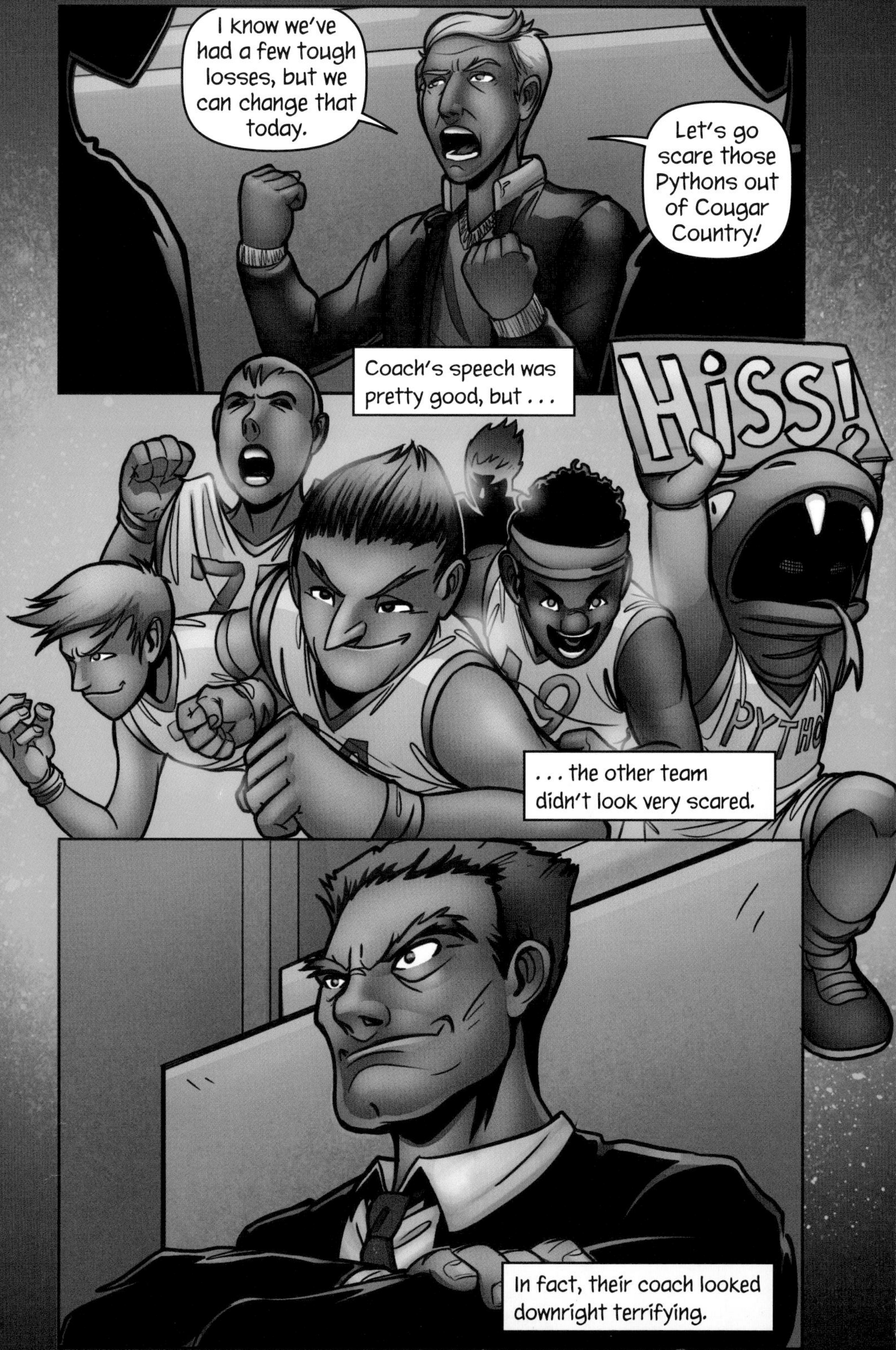
I know we've had a few tough losses, but we can change that today.
Let's go scare those Pythons out of Cougar Country!
Coach's speech was pretty good, but . . .
HiSS!
PYTHO
. . . the other team didn't look very scared.
In fact, their coach looked downright terrifying.

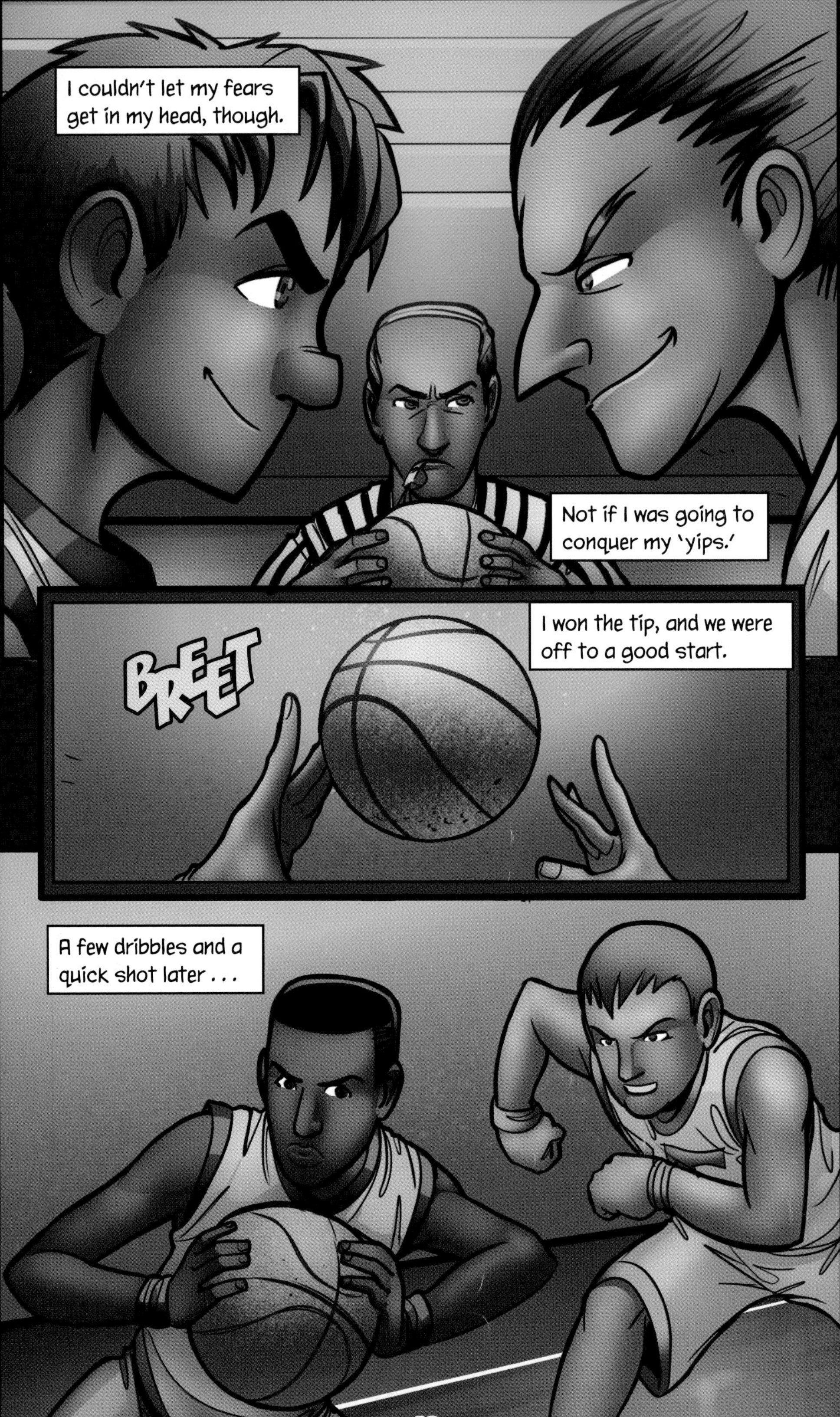
I couldn't let my fears get in my head, though.
Not if I was going to conquer my 'yips.'
BREET
I won the tip, and we were off to a good start.
A few dribbles and a quick shot later . . .

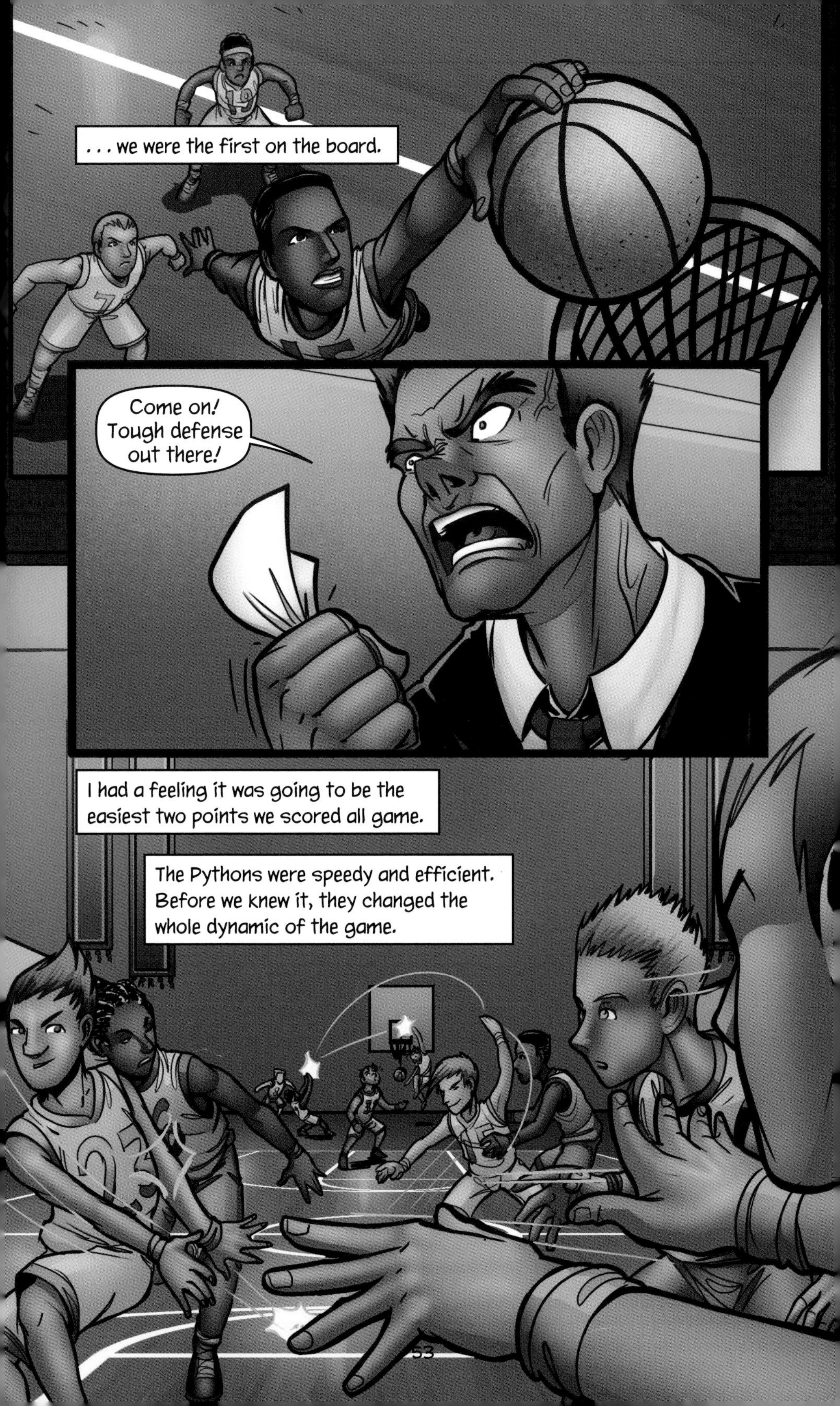
. . . we were the first on the board.
Come on! Tough defense out there!
I had a feeling it was going to be the easiest two points we scored all game.
The Pythons were speedy and efficient. Before we knew it, they changed the whole dynamic of the game.

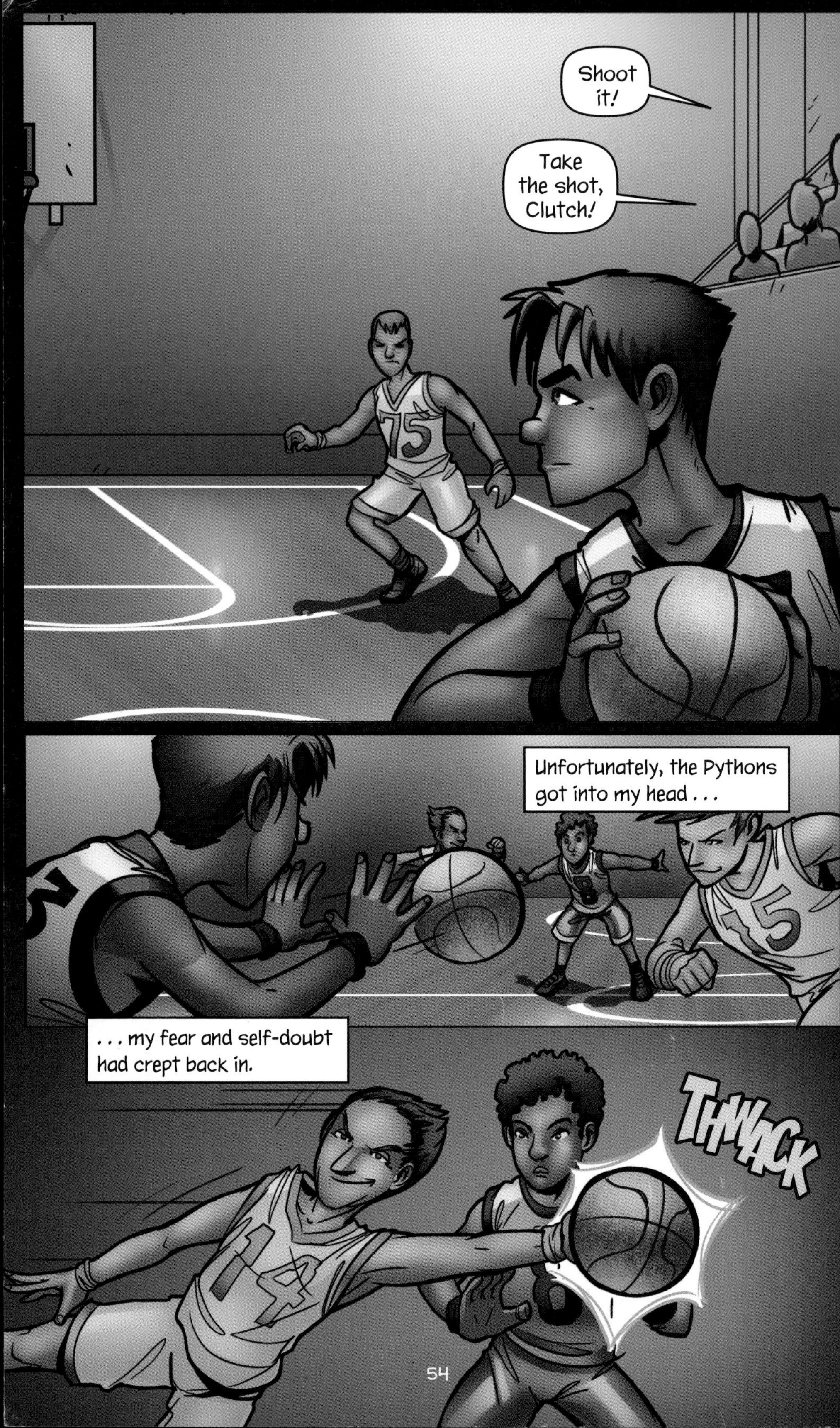
Shoot it!
Take the shot, Clutch!
Unfortunately, the Pythons got into my head . . .
. . . my fear and self-doubt had crept back in.
THWACK

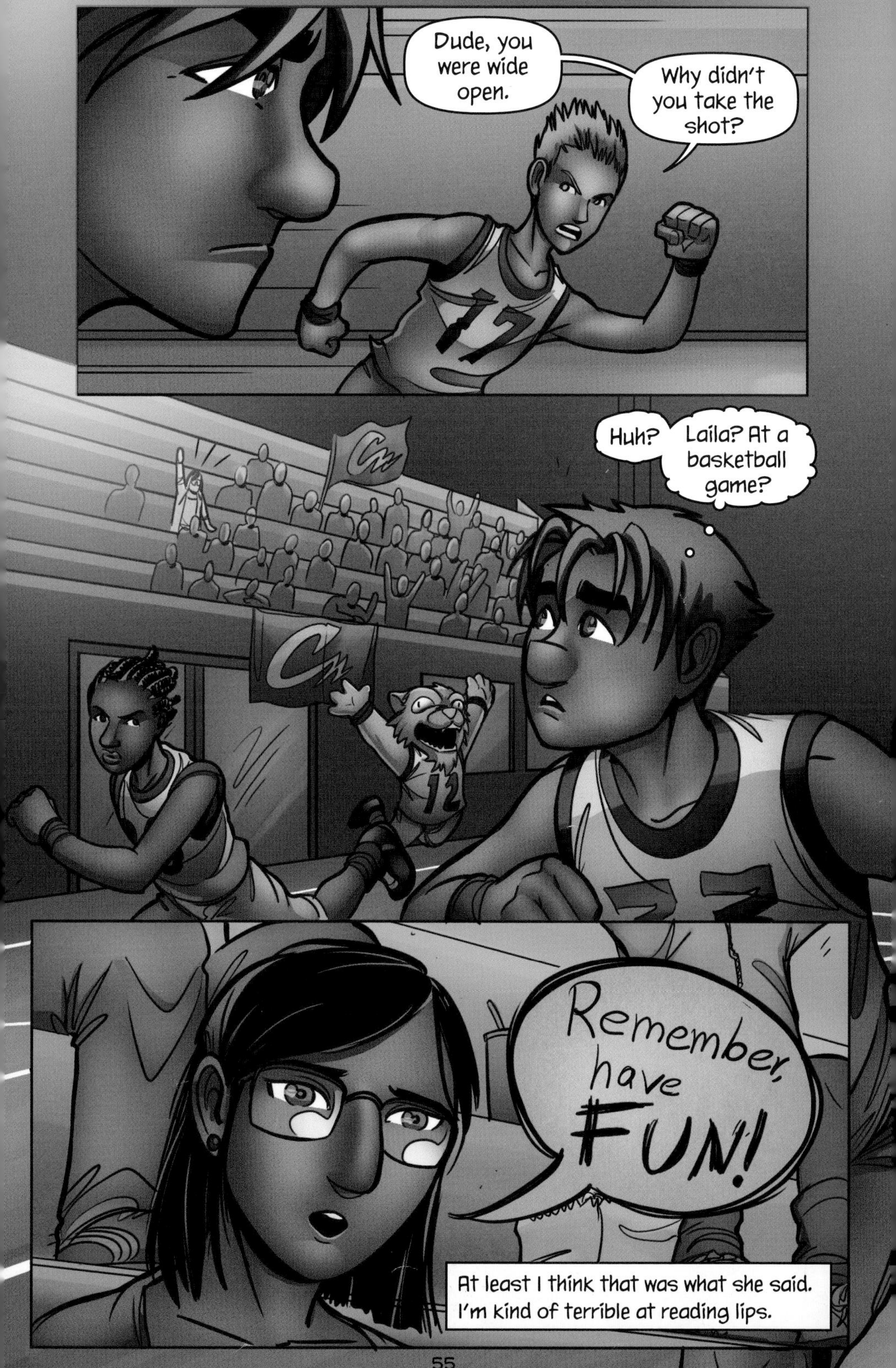
Dude, you were wide open.
Why didn't you take the shot?
Huh?
Laila? At a basketball game?
Remember, have FUN!
At least I think that was what she said. I'm kind of terrible at reading lips.

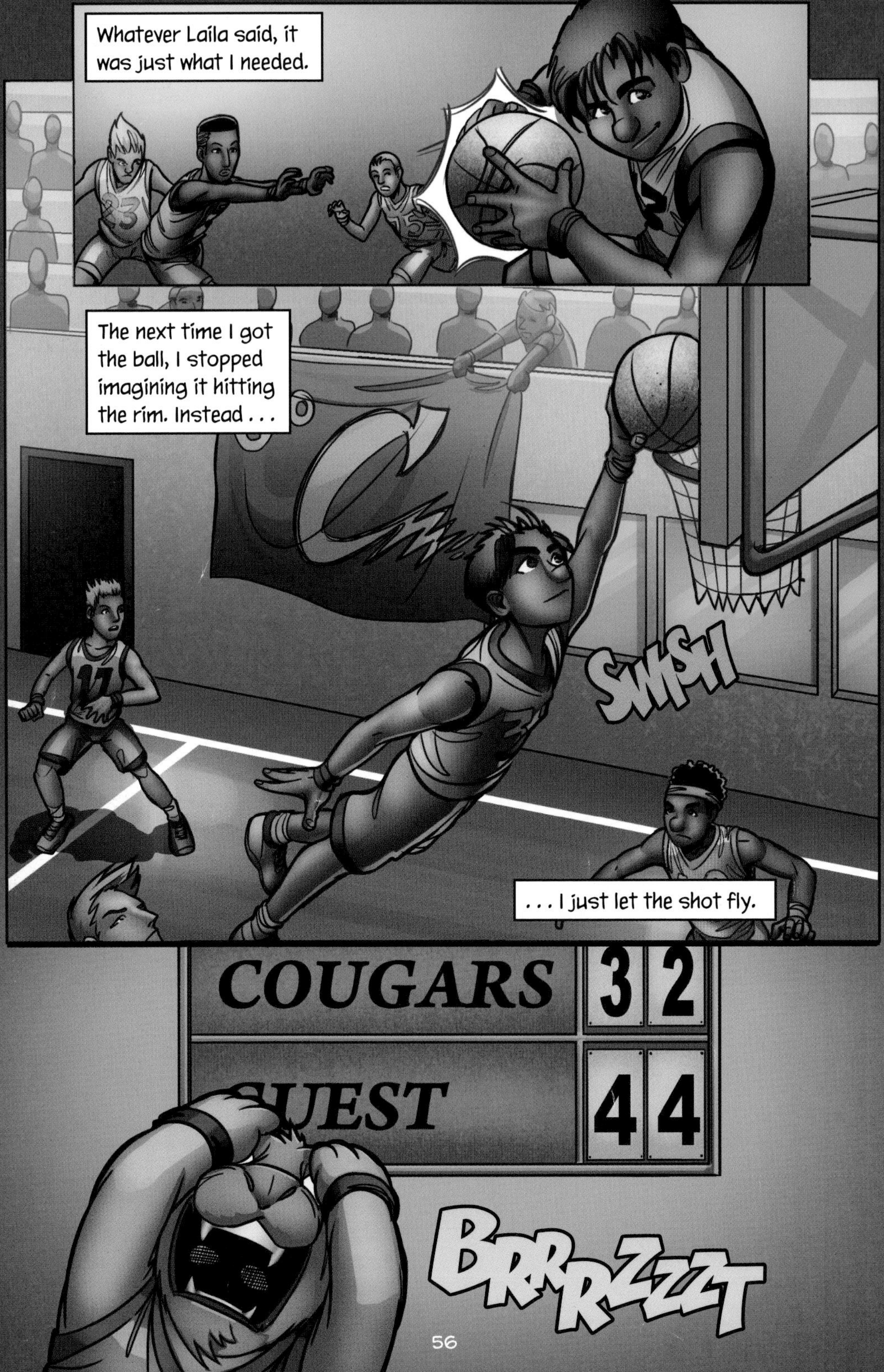
Whatever Laila said, it was just what I needed.
The next time I got the ball, I stopped imagining it hitting the rim. Instead . . .
SWISH
. . . I just let the shot fly.
COUGARS 32
GUEST 44
BRRRZZZT

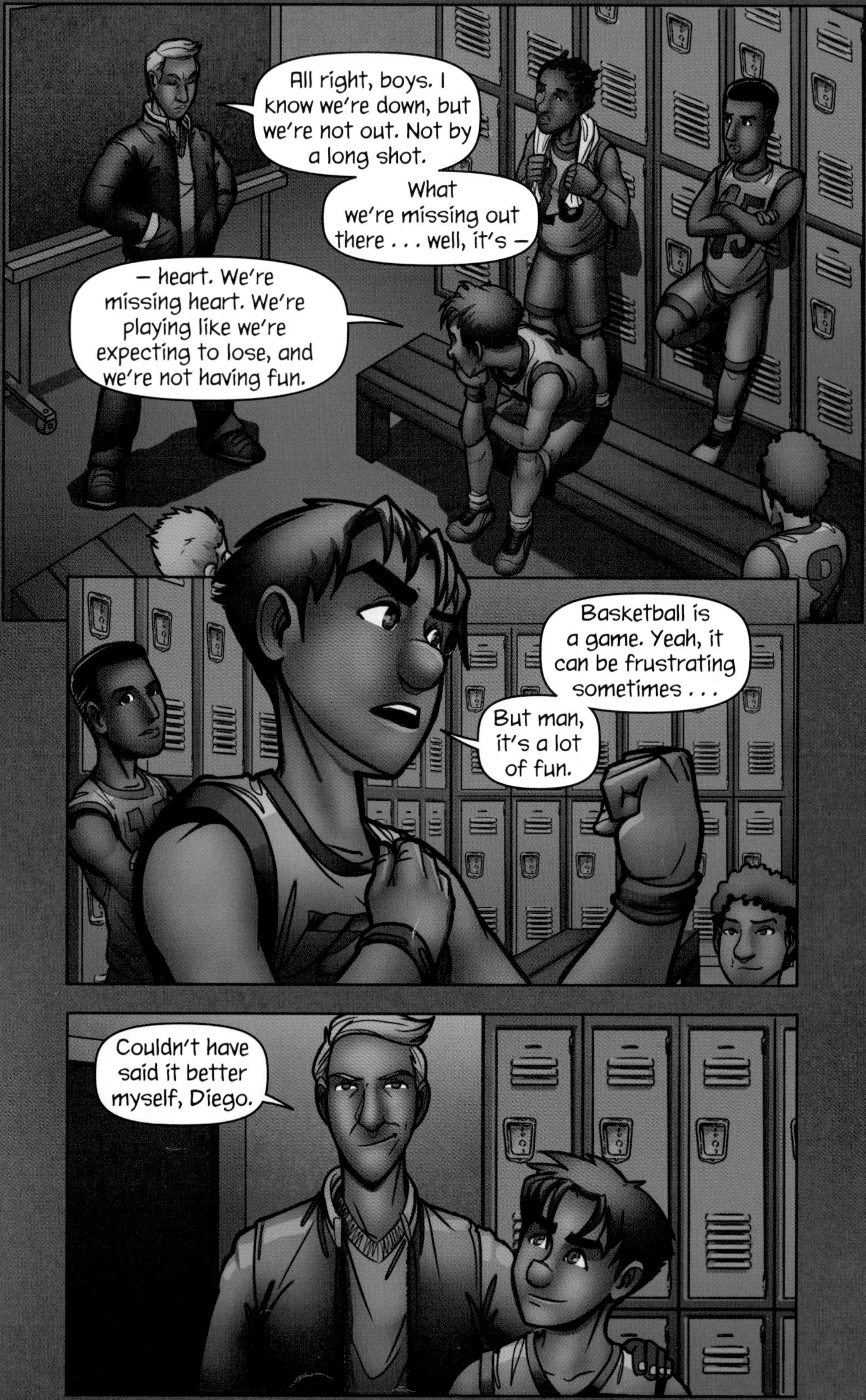
All right, boys. I know we're down, but we're not out. Not by a long shot.
What we're missing out there . . . well, it's —
— heart. We're missing heart. We're playing like we're expecting to lose, and we're not having fun.
Basketball is a game. Yeah, it can be frustrating sometimes . . .
But man, it's a lot of fun.
Couldn't have said it better myself, Diego.

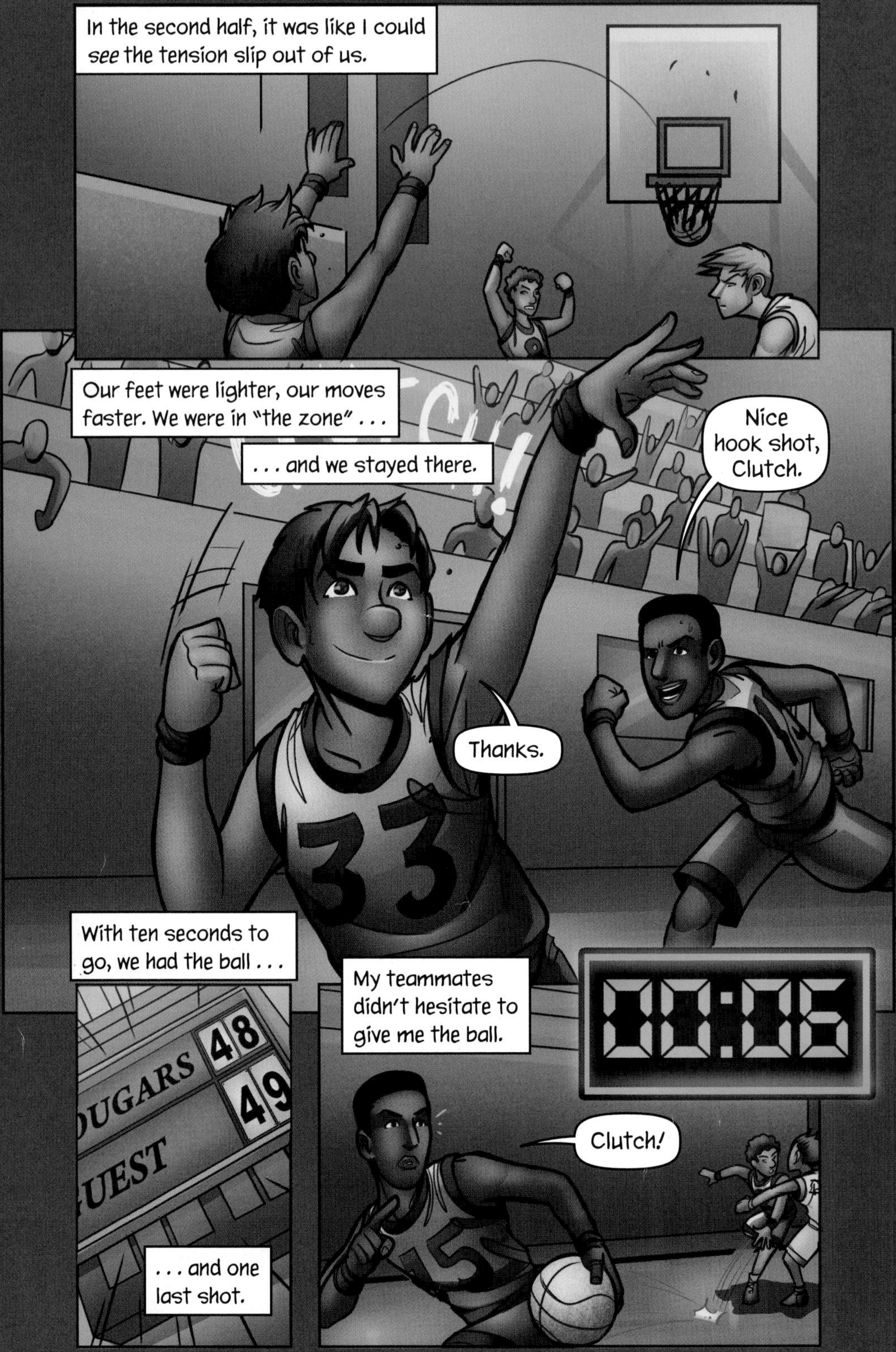
In the second half, it was like I could *see* the tension slip out of us.
Our feet were lighter, our moves faster. We were in "the zone" . . .
. . . and we stayed there.
Nice hook shot, Clutch.
Thanks.
With ten seconds to go, we had the ball . . .
OUGARS
UEST
48
49
. . . and one last shot.
My teammates didn't hesitate to give me the ball.
00:06
Clutch!

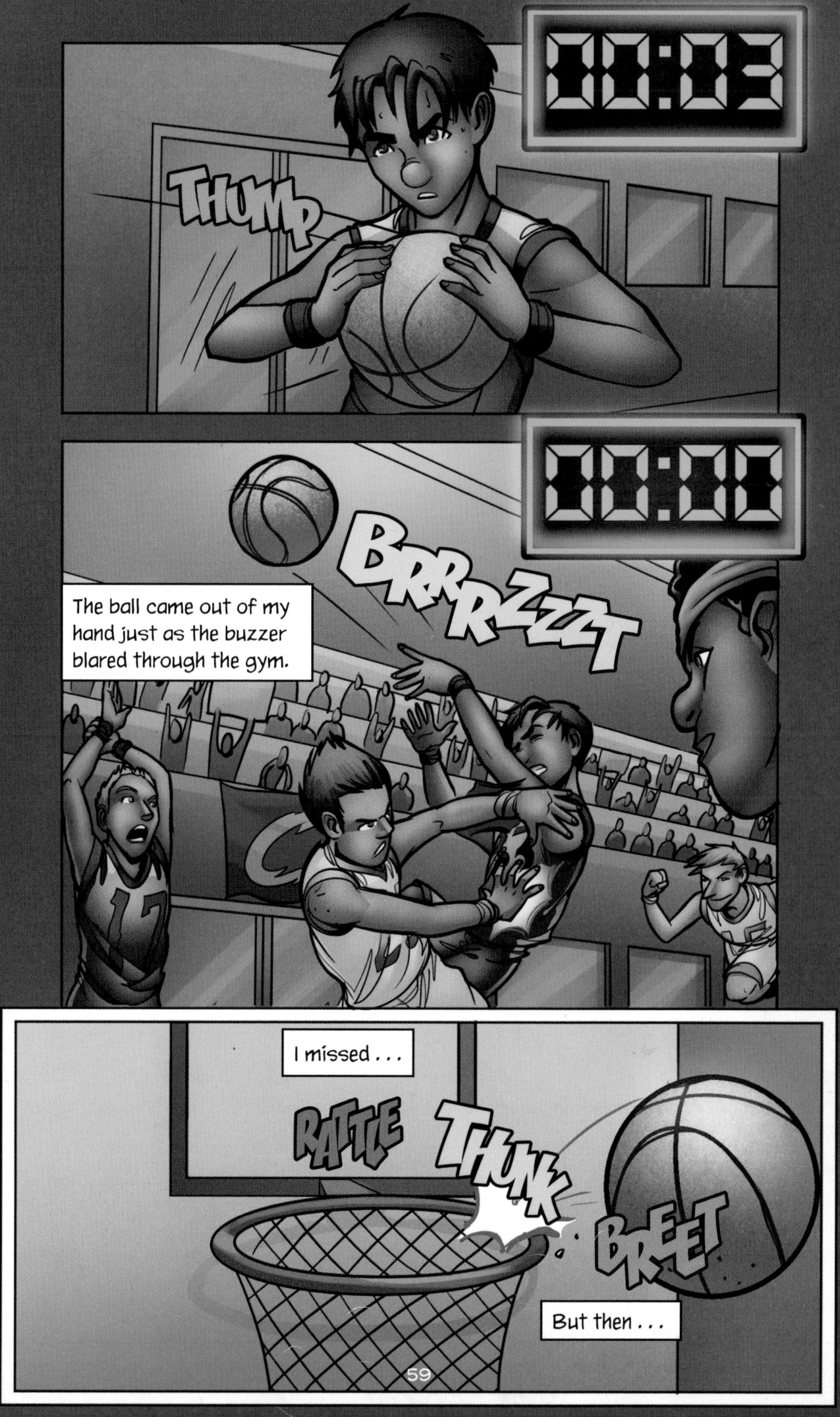
00:03
THUMP
00:00
BRRRZZZZT
The ball came out of my hand just as the buzzer blared through the gym.
I missed . . .
RATTLE
THUNK
BREET
But then . . .

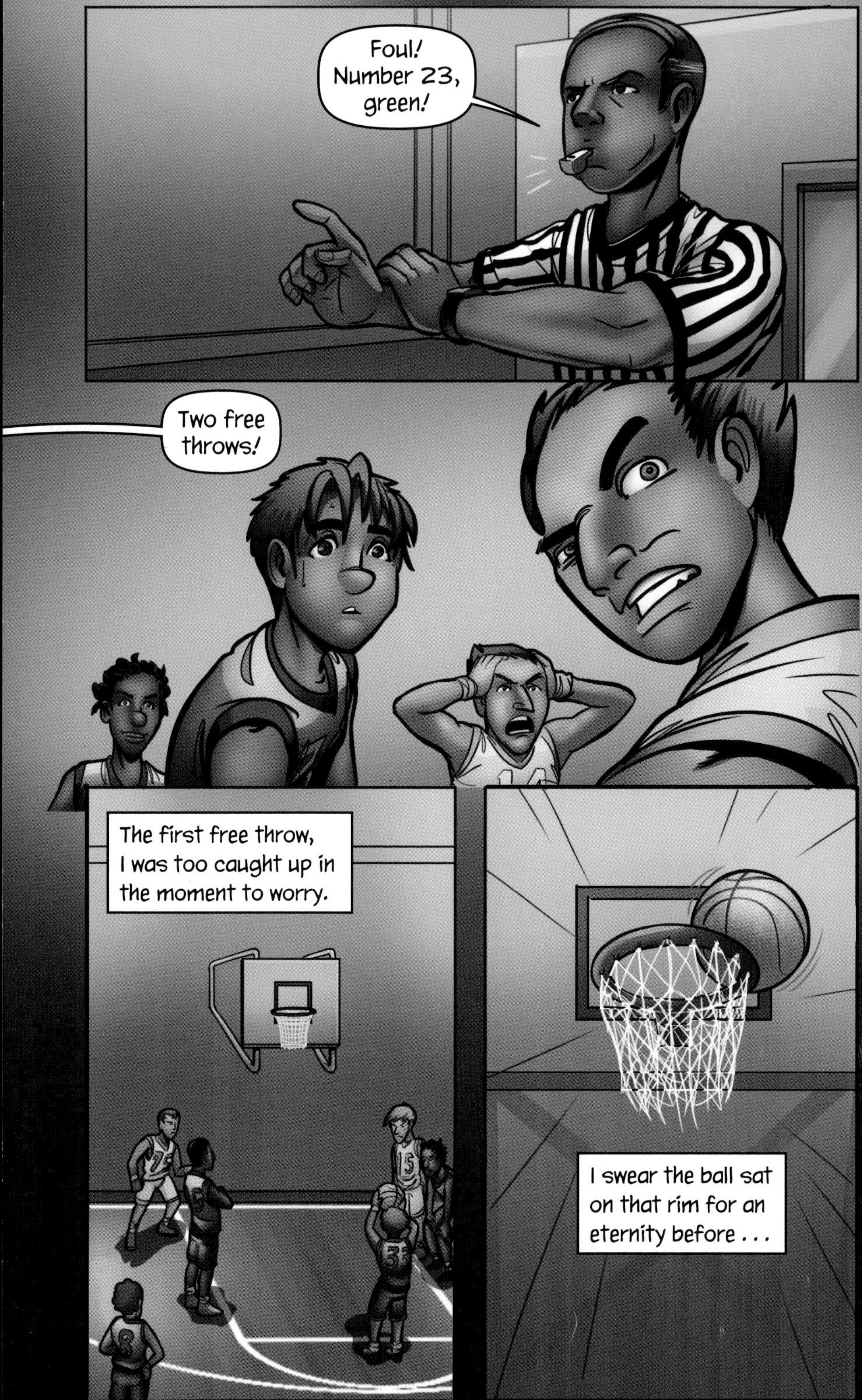
Foul! Number 23, green!
Two free throws!
The first free throw, I was too caught up in the moment to worry.
I swear the ball sat on that rim for an eternity before . . .

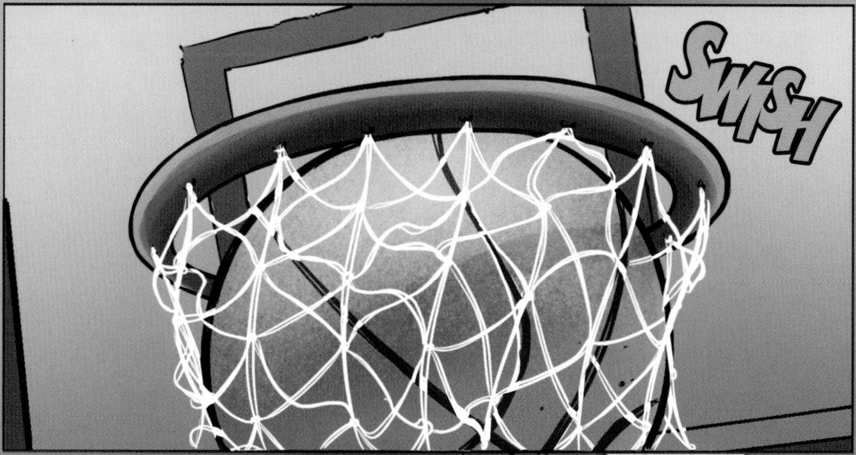
SWISH

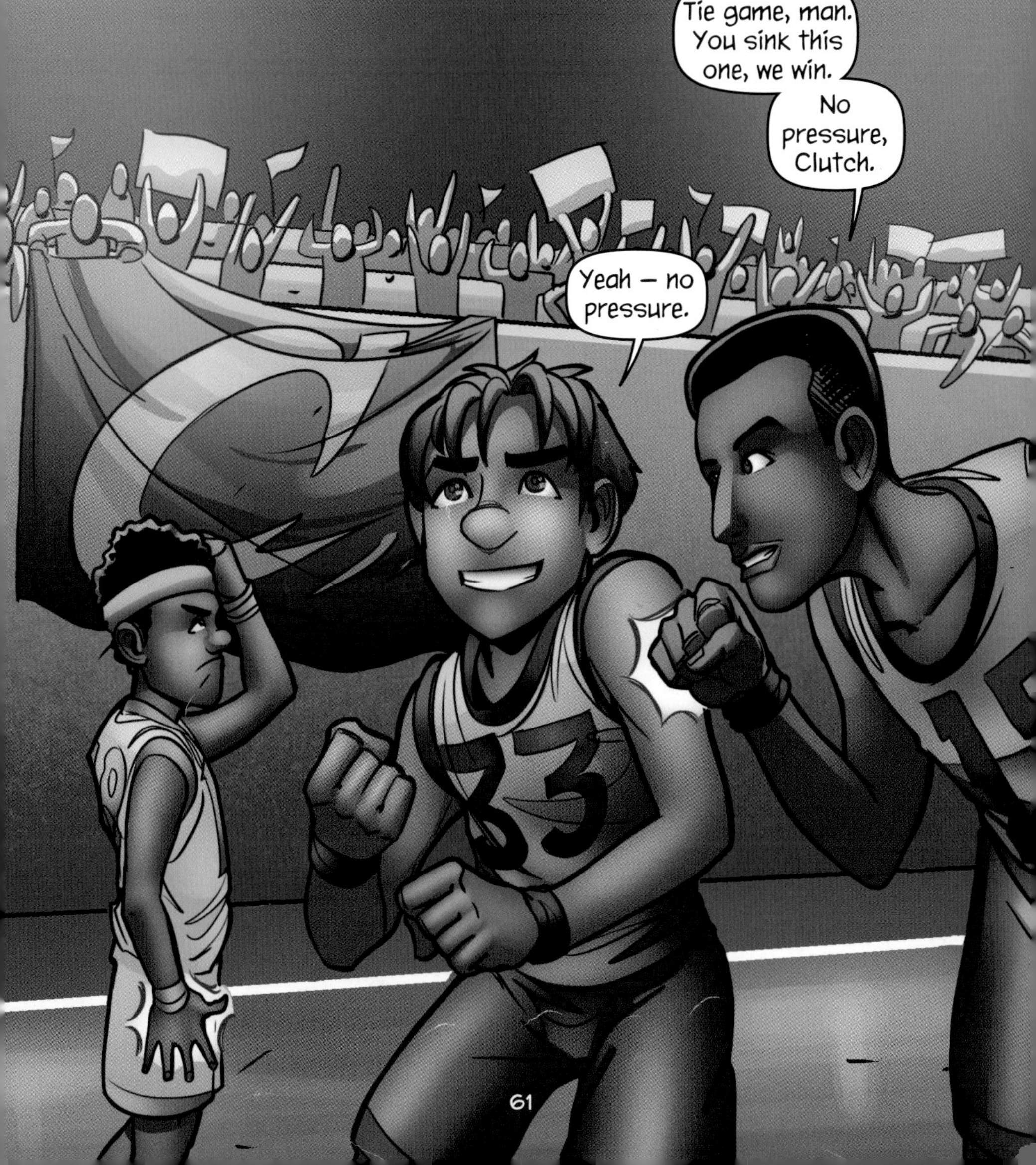
Tie game, man. You sink this one, we win.
No pressure, Clutch.
Yeah — no pressure.

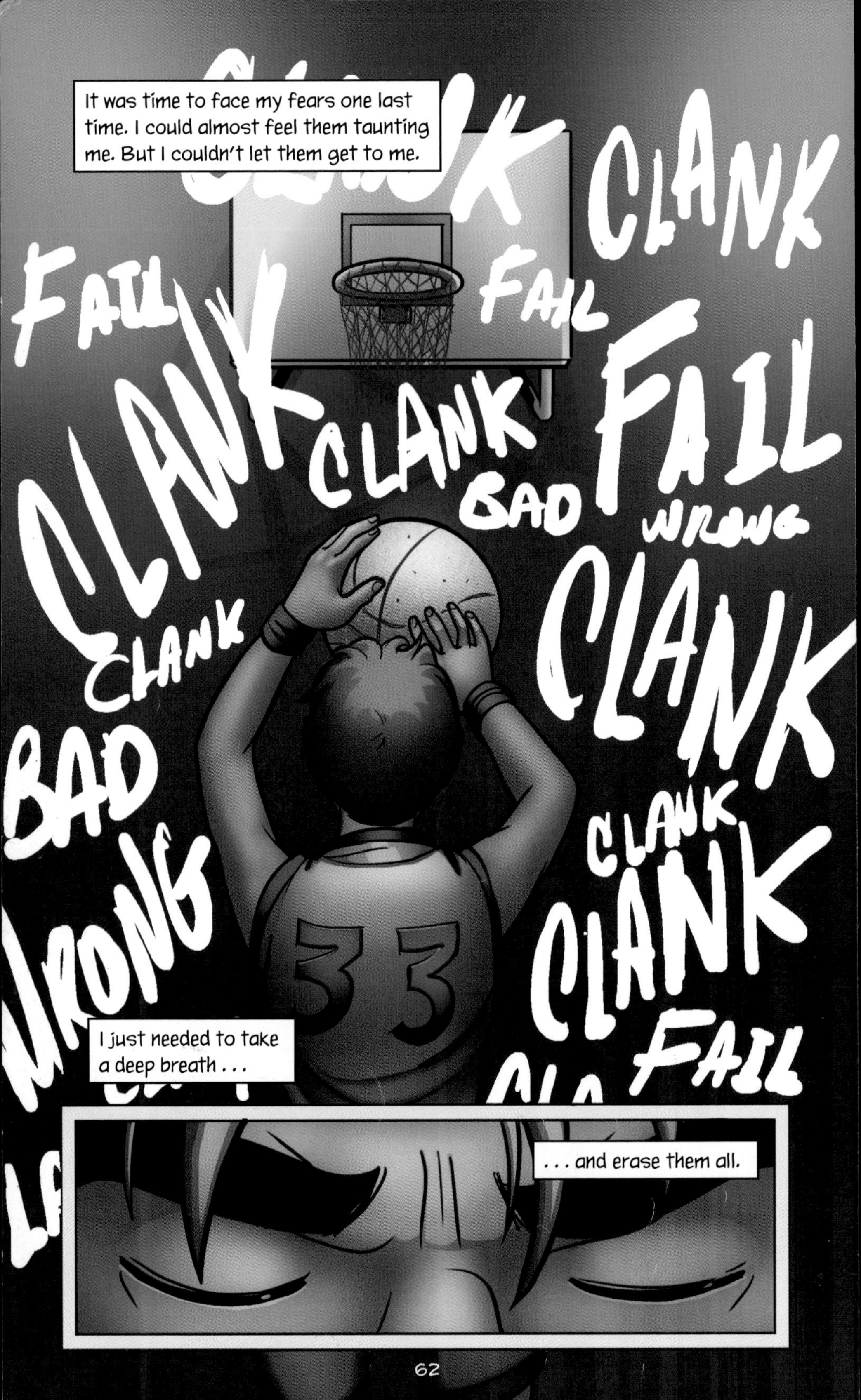
It was time to face my fears one last time. I could almost feel them taunting me. But I couldn't let them get to me.
CLANK
CLANK
FAIL
FAIL
CLANK
CLANK
FAIL
BAD
WRONG
CLANK
CLANK
BAD
CLANK
CLANK
WRONG
FAIL
I just needed to take a deep breath . . .
. . . and erase them all.

Leaving nothing but a blank page.

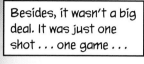

Besides, it wasn't a big deal. It was just one shot . . . one game . . .

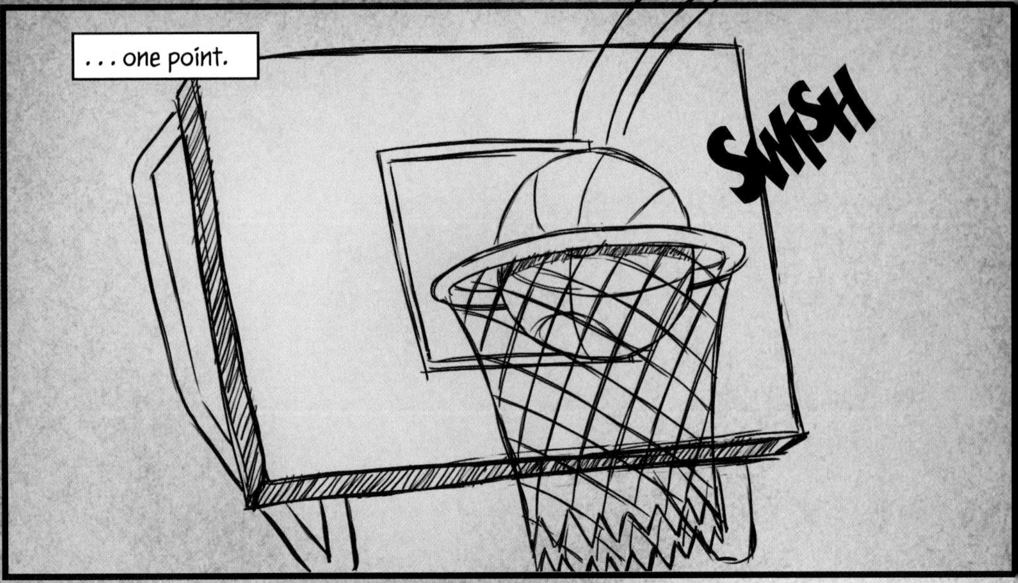
. . . one point.
SWISH

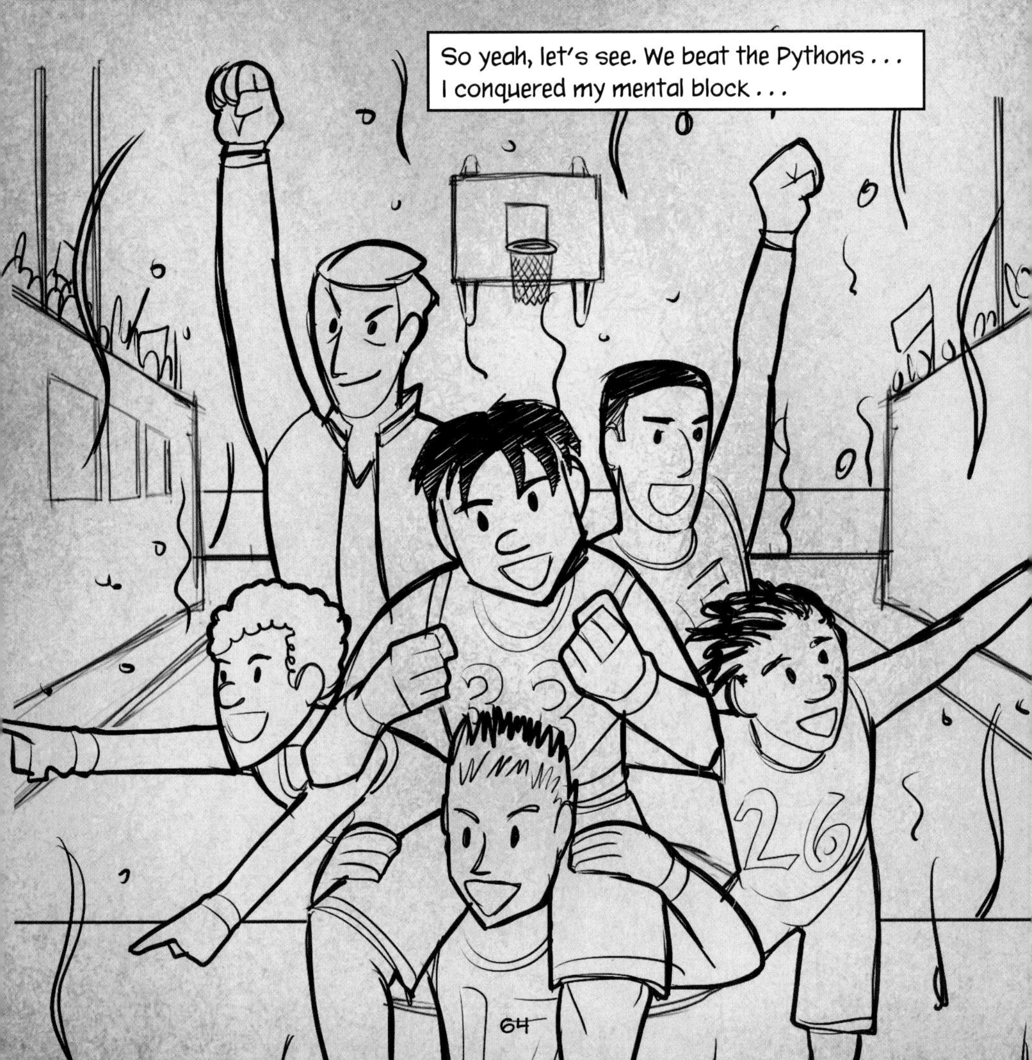
So yeah, let's see. We beat the Pythons . . .
I conquered my mental block . . .
33
26

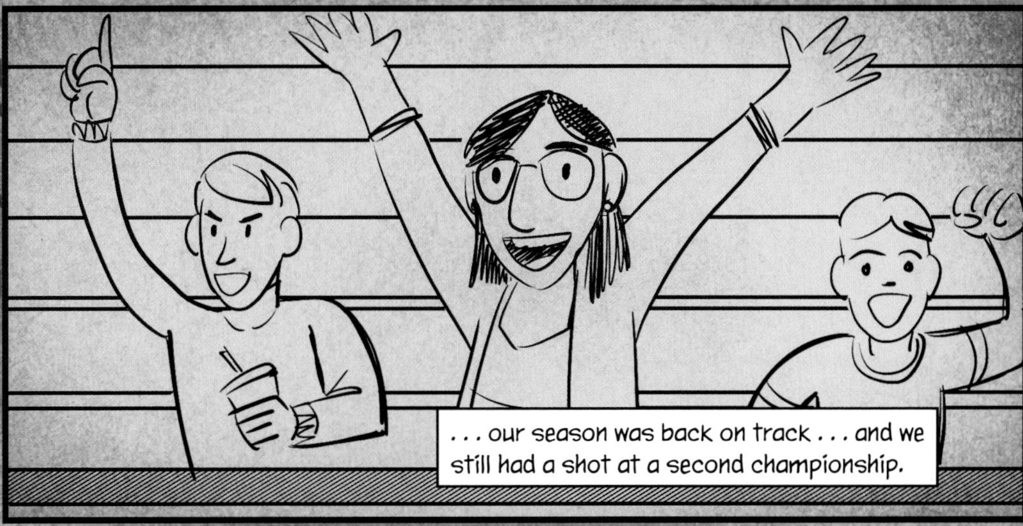
. . . our season was back on track . . . and we still had a shot at a second championship.

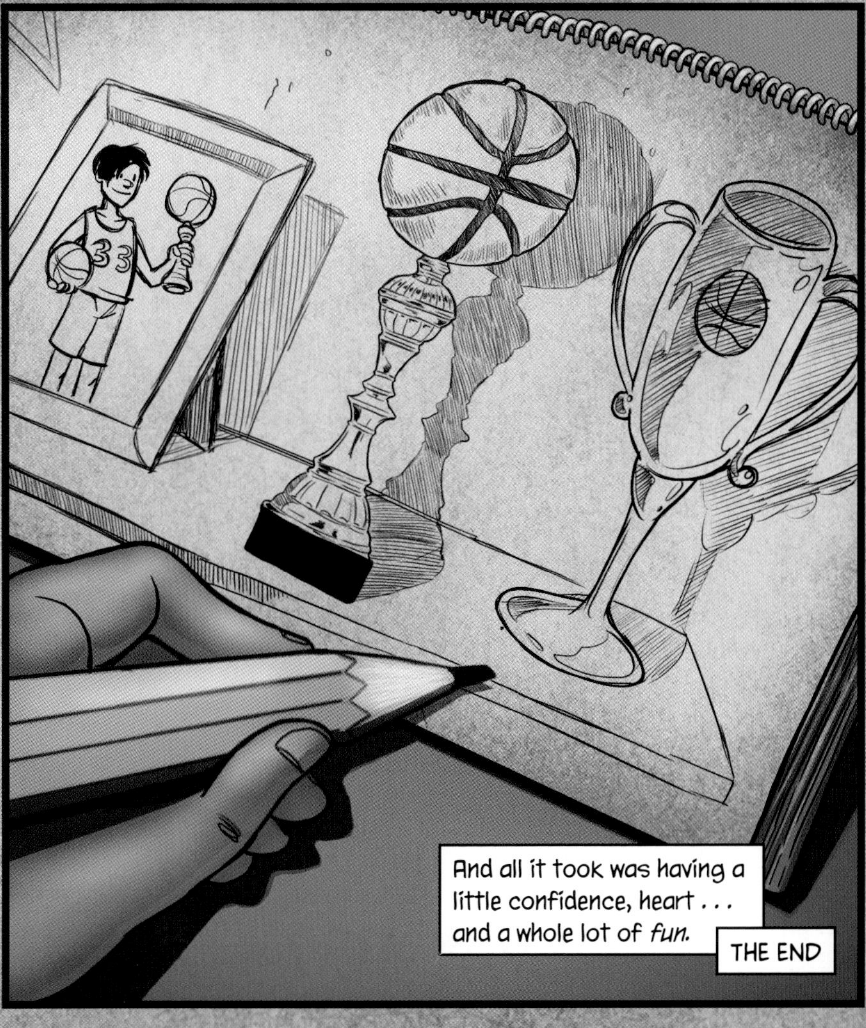
And all it took was having a little confidence, heart . . . and a whole lot of *fun.*
THE END

VISUAL QUESTIONS

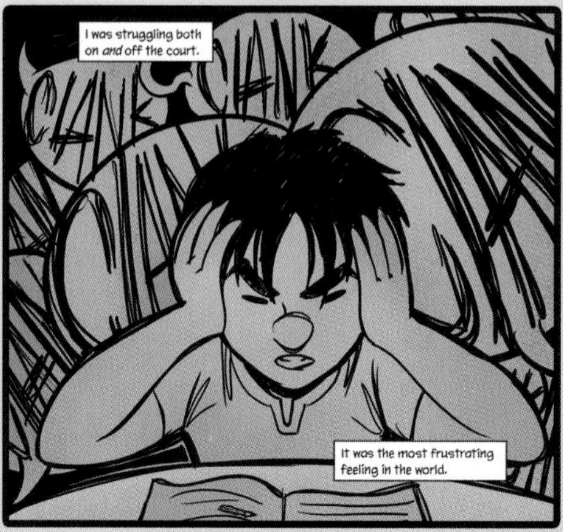
I was struggling both on *and* off the court.
It was the most frustrating feeling in the world.

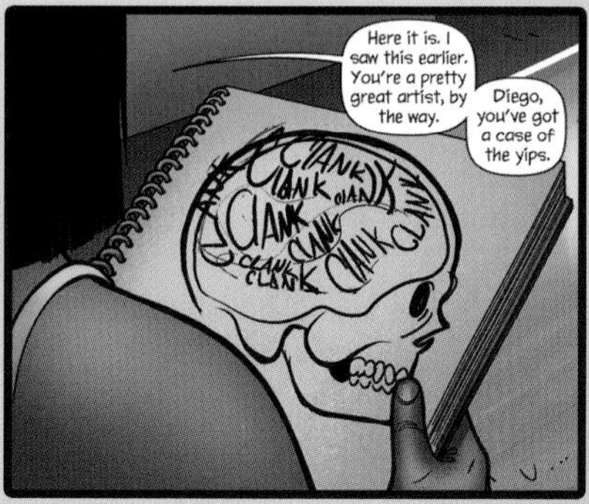
Here it is. I saw this earlier. You're a pretty great artist, by the way.
Diego, you've got a case of the yips.

1. In this story Diego used a sketchbook to draw out his feelings. Looking at these panels, what can you tell about Diego's feelings concerning his struggles on the basketball court?

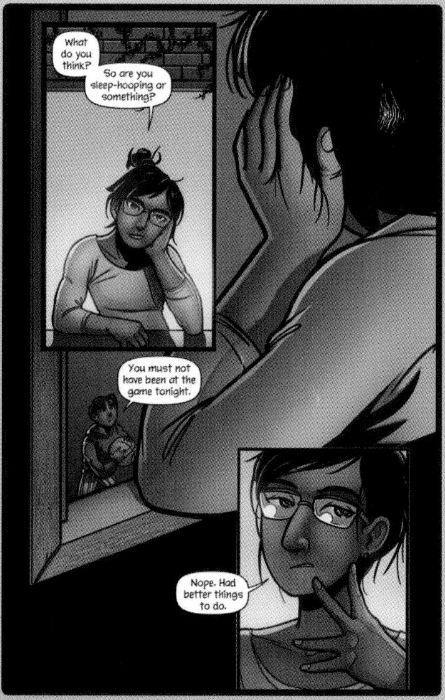
What do you think?
So are you sleep-hooping or something?
You must not have been at the game tonight.
Nope. Had better things to do.

2. Graphic artists often use different perspectives to tell a story. How do the panels to the right work together to show us the location of Diego and Laila as they talk to one another?

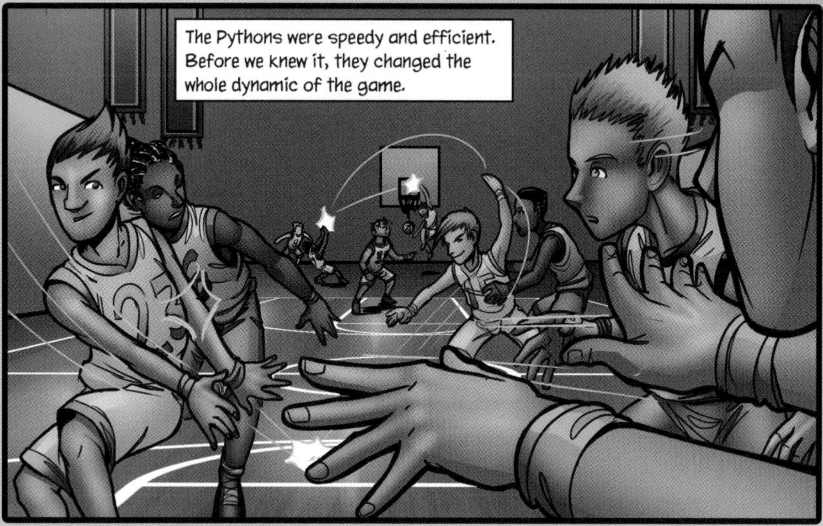
The Pythons were speedy and efficient. Before we knew it, they changed the whole dynamic of the game.

3. Graphic art can often show many parts of a story in a single panel. What does the above panel tell us about the Cougars' game against the Pythons?

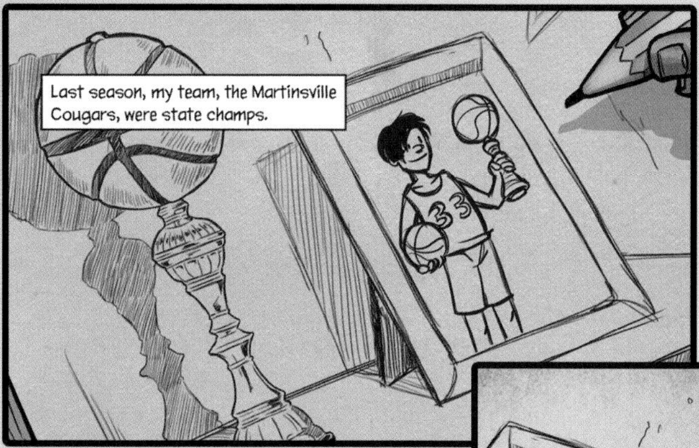
Last season, my team, the Martinsville Cougars, were state champs.

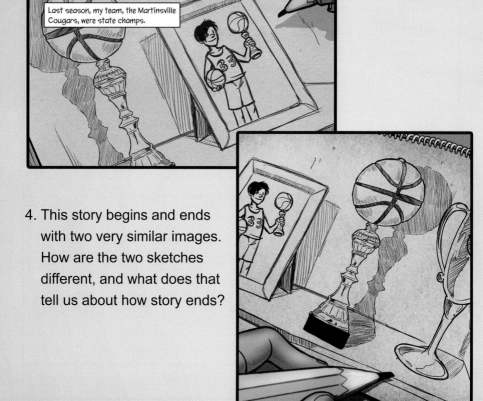

4. This story begins and ends with two very similar images. How are the two sketches different, and what does that tell us about how story ends?

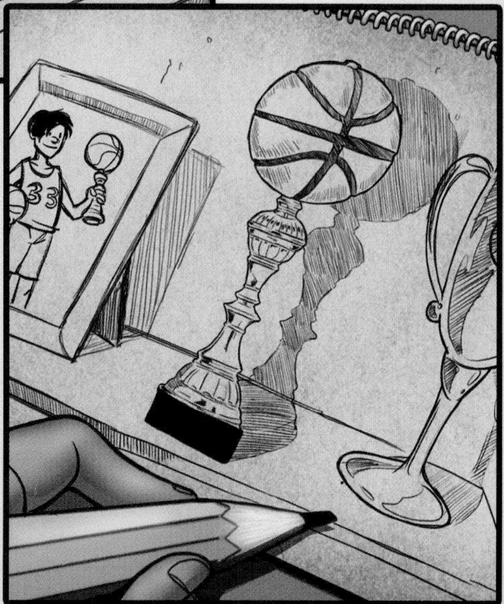

FUN BASKETBALL FACTS

1. Dr. James Naismith invented the game of basketball in 1891. He created it for athletes at his school in Springfield, Massachusetts who were bored in the winter. Each team had nine players. To score points, the players threw a soccer ball into peach baskets hung from the gym balcony.

2. Basketball was introduced as an Olympic sport at the 1936 Summer Games held in Berlin, Germany.

3. The National Basketball Association (NBA) was formed in 1946, but was originally called the Basketball Association of America. The league's first official game was played on November 1, 1946, between the Toronto Huskies and the New York Knickerbockers.

4. Philadelphia center Wilt Chamberlain scored a record 100 points in a single game on March 2, 1962.

5. Kareem Abdul Jabbar played for 20 seasons in the NBA. He holds the record for the most career points scored with 38,387.

6. The Boston Celtics have won a record 17 NBA championship titles. The Los Angeles Lakers are a close second with 16 total championships.

KNOW YOUR BASKETBALL TERMS

fast break — a quick offensive drive to the basket, attempting to beat the defense down the court

free throw — also known as a foul shot, free throws are awarded after a player is fouled by an opposing player; free throw shots are made from the foul line and are worth one point each

hook shot — a shot made by swinging your arm up and over your head

jump ball — a method of putting a basketball into play; the referee throws the ball into the air between two players, who jump up and try to direct it to one of their teammates

jump shot — a shot made while jumping and releasing the ball at the peak of your jump

layup — a shot made from very close to the basket, usually by bouncing the ball off the backboard

paint — the painted area on a basketball court underneath the basket where much of the action takes place

rebound — to catch the basketball after a shot has been missed

three-pointer — a successful shot from outside the designated arc of the three-point line on a basketball court

GLOSSARY

confidence (KON-fi-duhnss)—to believe in yourself and your own abilities

determined (dih-TUR-muhnd)—having a firm or fixed purpose

dynamic (dye-NAM-ik)—the changing atmosphere of a group of people participating in an activity

fluke (FLOOK)—a lucky or unlucky accident

full court press (FULL CORT PRESS)—in basketball, when a team's defense applies pressure to the offense for the entire length of the court

MVP (EM VEE PEE)—short for "most valuable player"

pep rally (PEP RAL-ee)—a meeting of students before an athletic event to build unity and show support for a team

pick (PIK)—when an offensive player blocks a defender to allow a teammate to shoot, receive a pass, or drive in to score

reputation (rep-yoo-TAY-shuhn)—a person's character as judged by other people

taunt (TAWNT)—to use words or actions to insult another person or make someone angry

tension (TEN-shuhn)—a feeling of stress, worry, or nervousness

yips (YIPS)—nervousness or tension that can destroy one's concentration, confidence, and performance

READ THEM ALL!

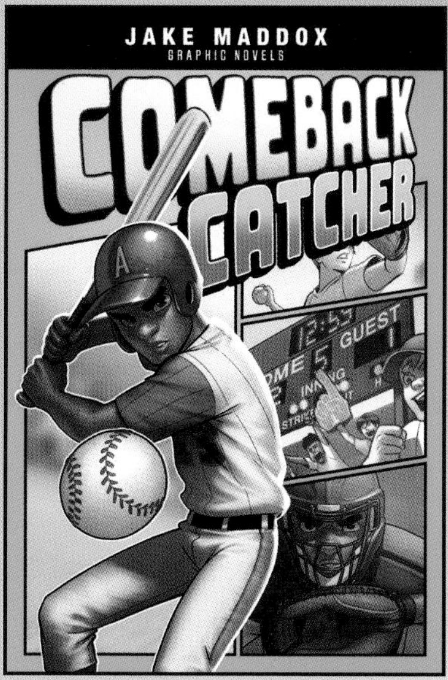
JAKE MADDOX
GRAPHIC NOVELS
COMEBACK CATCHER

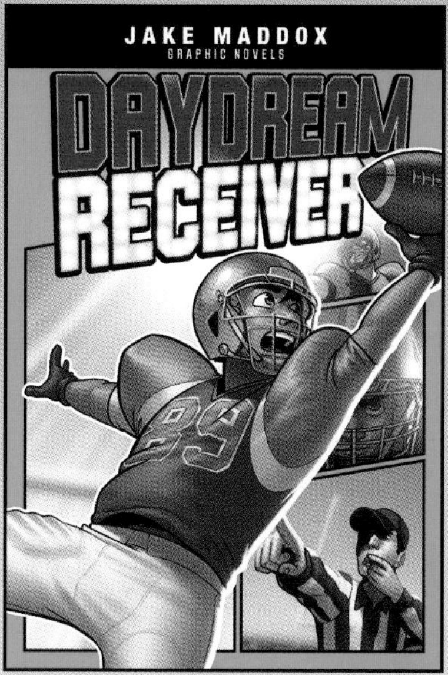
JAKE MADDOX
GRAPHIC NOVELS
DAYDREAM RECEIVER

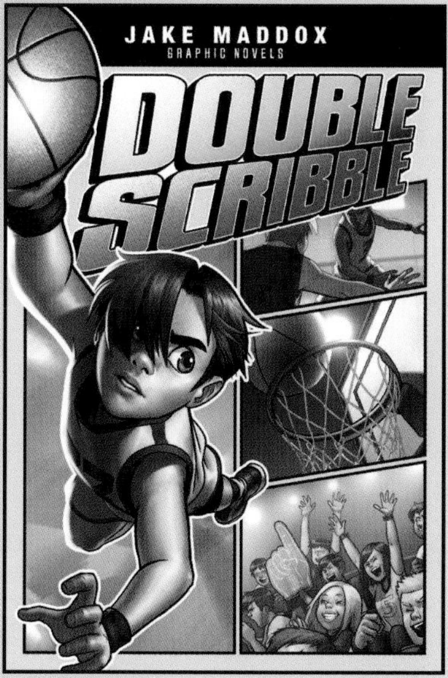
JAKE MADDOX
GRAPHIC NOVELS
DOUBLE SCRIBBLE

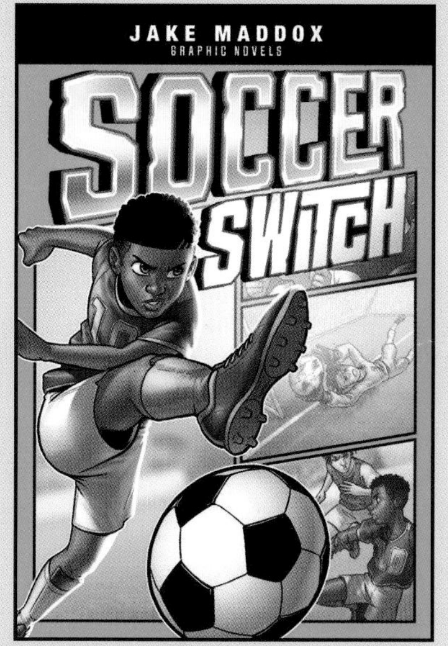
JAKE MADDOX
GRAPHIC NOVELS
SOCCER SWITCH

FIND OUT MORE AT
WWW.MYCAPSTONE.COM

ABOUT THE AUTHOR

Brandon Terrell is the author of numerous children's books, including six volumes in the Tony Hawk's 900 Revolution series and several Sports Illustrated Kids Graphic Novels. When not hunched over his laptop writing, Brandon enjoys watching movies, reading, watching and playing baseball, and spending time with his wife and two children in Minnesota.

ABOUT THE ILLUSTRATOR

Aburtov has worked in the comic book industry for more than eleven years. In that time, he has illustrated popular characters such as Wolverine, Iron Man, Blade, and the Punisher. Recently, Aburtov started his own illustration studio called Graphikslava. He lives in Monterrey, Mexico, with his daughter, Ilka, and his beloved wife. Aburtov enjoys spending his spare time with family and friends.